A CAMP SUNNYSIDE

Christmas Reunion

Katie's mother's eyes sparkled. "Call all your friends from Cabin Six, and invite them here for a visit. They can come on Monday and stay until New Year's Day."

Katie was speechless. She stared at her mother in disbelief. It took a full minute for her to absorb what her mother was saying. And then she couldn't even respond properly. All she could do was jump up and down and shriek with joy!

THIS WAS GOING TO BE
THE BEST CHRISTMAS VACATION EVER!

Happy Holidays from the Girls in Cabin Six!

Look for More Fun and Games with
CAMP SUNNYSIDE FRIENDS
by Marilyn Kaye
from Avon Books

(#1) NO BOYS ALLOWED!
(#2) CABIN SIX PLAYS CUPID
(#3) COLOR WAR!
(#4) NEW GIRL IN CABIN SIX
(#5) LOOKING FOR TROUBLE
(#6) KATIE STEALS THE SHOW
(#7) A WITCH IN CABIN SIX
(#8) TOO MANY COUNSELORS
(#9) THE NEW-AND-IMPROVED SARAH

And Don't Miss
MY CAMP MEMORY BOOK
the delightful souvenir album for
recording camp memories and planning activities

Coming Soon

(#10) ERIN AND THE MOVIE STAR

MARILYN KAYE is the author of many popular books for young readers, including the "Out of This World" series and the "Sisters" books. She is an associate professor at St. John's University and lives in Brooklyn, New York.

Camp Sunnyside is the camp Marilyn Kaye wishes that she had gone to every summer when she was a kid.

SPECIAL

Christmas Reunion

Marilyn Kaye

AN AVON CAMELOT BOOK

CAMP SUNNYSIDE FRIENDS SPECIAL: CHRISTMAS REUNION
is an original publication of Avon Books. This work has never before
appeared in book form.

AVON BOOKS
A division of
The Hearst Corporation
105 Madison Avenue
New York, New York 10016

First Avon Camelot Printing: December 1990

CAMELOT TRADEMARK REG. U.S. PAT. OFF. AND IN OTHER COUNTRIES, MARCA
REGISTRADA, HECHO EN U.S.A.

Printed in the U.S.A.

OPM 10 9 8 7 6 5 4 3 2 1

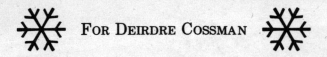 FOR DEIRDRE COSSMAN

Chapter 1

"Katie, would you please pick up all this stuff?" Mrs. Dillon surveyed the wads of brightly colored paper, ribbons, and empty boxes that surrounded the Christmas tree.

Katie was setting the time on her new watch. "In a minute, Mom."

"Now." Mrs. Dillon's voice was firm. "I asked you to do that an hour ago."

Katie gazed at the mess on the floor in dismay. "You want me to pick up all that wrapping paper?"

Mrs. Dillon nodded. "Put it in this garbage bag."

"Ribbons, too?"

"Everything."

Sighing, Katie put her watch down on the coffee table and got up. "Why can't Peter or Michael do this?" she grumbled as she started gathering the scraps from the floor.

"Because I asked *you* to," her mother said

briskly. "And anyway, they're loading the dishwasher."

That was some comfort, Katie thought. At least, they had the harder job. It had been an enormous Christmas dinner—turkey and all the stuff that went with it. And that meant a lot of dishes for her brothers to scrape.

"And I'd be very grateful if you'd run the vacuum over the rug when you're done," Mrs. Dillon added over her shoulder as she headed upstairs.

Katie's brief moment of satisfaction faded. Vacuuming had to be her least favorite job in the world. Some Christmas, she thought, tossing an armful of wrapping paper into the garbage bag and crushing it down to make room for more. If they were at Gramma's, where they were *supposed* to be, she wouldn't be doing chores. But Gramma had decided to escape the cold Pennsylvania winter and visit friends in Florida.

Not that Christmas here had been bad. Great gifts, good food, and the tree was beautiful—even if it wasn't exactly the way Katie had wanted it to look. She'd made an angel out of colored paper and tin foil to go on top. But her brothers had insisted on their traditional star, even though it was pretty shabby looking. And her parents had agreed with them. She had to stick her angel on the tree like a regular ornament.

Okay, it was no big deal. But it annoyed her that Peter and Michael always seemed to get their way. Like last night, when the carolers came by. The family had gathered at the open door to listen. When the carolers asked for any requests, Katie called out for "Hark, the Herald Angels Sing." But Peter and Michael, whose voices were louder, demanded "Joy to the World," and that's what the carolers sang.

Katie went to the closet and dragged out the vacuum cleaner. She grimaced at the roar of the machine when she turned it on. Or maybe she was just still thinking about her brothers.

They even got their way when it came to food. Just yesterday when her mother had been making the grocery list for Christmas dinner, she'd asked what they preferred for dessert—lemon meringue pie or chocolate cream. Katie had spoken up for lemon meringue, but the boys wanted chocolate cream. She'd been outvoted. But she was *always* outvoted. There were two of them and only one of her. A long time ago, she pointed out to her mother that the boys should only have one vote, since they were twins. Her idea was turned down.

It was only dessert. Like the angel, it was no big deal. She would have lost even if the twins

3

did have one vote, since her father had also opted for chocolate cream. And it wasn't as if she didn't like chocolate cream almost as much as lemon meringue. But still—it was just one more example of the boys getting their way.

She switched off the vacuum.

"Hey!"

She turned and saw the twins. "What?"

Peter pointed to a place on the rug. "You missed a spot."

Katie squinted. "I can't even see it."

"*I* can see it," Michael said sternly. "And if I can see it, Mom will see it. So you better vacuum it up."

Katie glared at them. She didn't know what annoyed her more—when they teased her or when they ordered her around. Either way, they were a pain.

"Let's play Ping-Pong," Peter said to Michael, and they headed toward the basement stairs. Angrily, Katie switched the vacuum back on. The Ping-Pong table had been a Christmas gift for all of them. But she could guess who'd be monopolizing it.

Finally, she finished vacuuming, and went to the closet to put the cleaner away.

"Nice job, honey." Her father stood in the doorway.

"Thanks," Katie said dully. It wasn't very

thrilling to be complimented for a good vacuuming job.

Mr. Dillon gazed at her curiously. "Something bothering you?"

There was no point in declaring her complaints about the twins. Both her parents had heard them many times before. And it probably wasn't right to complain on Christmas Day. "No, everything's fine."

He didn't look convinced. "Just the usual post-Christmas letdown, huh? Well, you've got a whole week of vacation left. That's something to look forward to."

Katie looked at him hopefully. "Dad, could we go somewhere? Like, skiing up in Vermont?"

He shook his head with regret. "Not this year, Katie. I can't get away from the office. Now, don't look so disappointed. You can have plenty of fun right here in town with your friends." He yawned. "I'm going to have a nap."

He left the room, and Katie sat down on the floor next to the tree. She pulled up her knees, rested her elbows on them, and plunked her chin in her hands. Fun right here in town? That was easy for her father to say. How was she going to have any fun when none of her friends was around? They were all out of town, on vacations or visiting relatives. She certainly couldn't plan on having much fun here at home, not with her

5

brothers. Even if she wanted to hang out with them, they wouldn't want her around.

She could sense a gloomy cloud about to descend on her head. To ward it off, she started going through her presents again. She had to admit, she'd done really well this year. There was the watch, and she'd also gotten two sweaters, a scarf and mitten set, ice skates, and a clock radio. In addition, there were four albums, a puzzle with a zillion pieces, and the brand-new board game, Wacko, that everyone was playing.

And then there was her present from Gramma. When the box arrived in the mail, she couldn't imagine what it was. It was so *big*. At first, she fantasized about a television, a new stereo—something like that—but the box wasn't heavy enough. She certainly didn't expect what she saw when she opened it that morning.

It was a doll. Not just a regular doll, like a baby doll or a Barbie. It was almost as tall as Katie. And she was gorgeous, with yellow curls cascading down her back. She was dressed in a very elegant velvet gown.

The twins had hooted when Katie pulled the doll out of the box. And her mother had smiled ruefully. "I guess Gramma still thinks you're a little girl, Katie."

Gazing at the doll now, Katie had to admit a doll hadn't been on her Christmas wish list. She was almost twelve, and she hadn't played with dolls in ages. She certainly didn't intend to play with this one.

But she didn't mind looking at her. There was something about the doll that Katie found strangely appealing. Maybe it was her sweet smile, or her eyes, so blue they looked like sapphires. The eyes reminded her of someone. Oh yeah, she thought, Erin Chapman had eyes that color.

Thinking of Erin made her think of Trina, Megan, Sarah, and Camp Sunnyside. What great times they'd all had in cabin six! They'd been there together every summer since they were eight years old. Their faces passed through her mind, each so different and unique.

And Katie herself was a different person at Camp Sunnyside. She was a leader. The others listened to her. They loved her ideas, and they asked for her advice. No one teased her or ordered her around. She sighed wistfully. Those were the days. It would be six long months before she saw Camp Sunnyside and her camp friends again.

She began gathering her gifts to carry them up to her room. It took two trips, since the doll alone was an armful. Up in her room, she set the doll on her bookcase, and put the other gifts away.

7

Then she started feeling blue again. To distract herself, she decided to re-read the letter Trina had written her.

Dear Katie,

I was so happy to get your last letter. I miss you too. With Christmas coming, I should be happy, but instead I'm feeling down. This will be the first Christmas since my parents got divorced. They have been arguing over who I'm supposed to spend Christmas Day with. They said it was my decision. I told them I wanted to stay here with Mom. But now I think my father feels really bad about that. I wish you were here. I need a friend to talk to.

Poor Trina. Katie too wished they could be together. She could always cheer Trina up and talk her out of being depressed about her parents.

Rummaging through her desk drawer, she pulled out the album of photos from last summer. Her mother appeared in her doorway.

"Thanks for cleaning up the living room, Katie. What are you doing?"

"Looking at my Sunnyside pictures."

Mrs. Dillon peered over her shoulder. "I haven't seen your cabin mates since the last Visitors'

Day. You'll have to refresh my memory. Who is that?"

Katie couldn't help smiling at the image of the small, red-haired girl who was grinning mischievously at the camera. "That's Megan." Even though her mother had heard all about her cabin mates, Katie felt a need to talk about them. "She's got the wildest imagination. I have to watch out for her, or she gets completely carried away. Like, when Carolyn, our counselor, broke up with her boyfriend, Teddy. Megan got it in her head that they were still madly in love, and she went crazy trying to get them back together. She made up all these stories about Carolyn, and practically got her fired."

"Yes, I remember you telling me about that," her mother said.

Katie tried to think of another example of Megan's imagination. "We had this day camper, Tanya. Megan decided she was a witch, and she was casting spells on us. She thought she was the only one who could save us from her."

Mrs. Dillon laughed. "She certainly has an imagination."

"No kidding. Megan's a real nut. But lots of fun."

She turned to the next photo. "That's Sarah."

"How can you tell?" her mother asked. All that could be seen of the person in the picture

9

were the upper edge of her eyeglass frames and some long brown hair. Her face was covered by the book she was holding.

"Sarah reads all the time," Katie explained. "She doesn't much like sports. I have to push her all the time to do things with us." She gazed at the picture thoughtfully. "She's got a big heart, though. There was a time last summer when we had this girl, Ms. Winkle's niece, staying with us for a while. She was kind of mean, and nobody liked her. And some kids thought she was stealing things. But Sarah kept defending her, and saying the girl was just putting on an act because she was unhappy. And Sarah was right."

"She sounds like a nice girl. And who's this?" Mrs. Dillon pointed to another picture. "She doesn't look twelve. Is she one of the counselors?"

Katie grinned. "No, that's Erin. I remember when I took that picture. She was all dressed up for this get-together at Camp Eagle across the lake."

"She looks so much older than the rest of you kids here."

"Yeah, and she never lets us forget it. She thinks she's so beautiful and sophisticated. She's always trying to get the rest of us to wear makeup and fix our hair. She did a whole makeover on Sarah once. And she made her miserable!"

"Does she get along with the rest of you?"

"Sometimes. But she's always telling us how immature we are. She wants to hang around with the older girls in cabin nine. Once, they tried to get her involved in this scheme to get rid of one of their cabin mates. She would have gotten into big trouble if I hadn't talked her out of it." She turned the page. "There's our counselor, Carolyn."

"You like her, don't you?"

"Yeah, she's okay for a counselor. I guess we should appreciate her more than we do." She laughed as a memory flooded her mind. "Once, she had to leave camp for a couple of weeks. We had these awful substitute counselors. We were a lot nicer to Carolyn when she came back!"

"This picture looks interesting," Mrs. Dillon said.

"That's me and Trina during color war."

"You were captain of your team, weren't you?"

Katie nodded. "Trina was on the other side." She bit her lip as she remembered something she'd never told her family—how she'd tried to get Trina to lose events on purpose so Katie's team could win. Thinking about it made her feel

11

ashamed. But Trina had forgiven her, and they were still best friends at Sunnyside.

"You know, it's weird," she told her mother. "We all live in Pennsylvania, and we figured out once that no one lives more than three hours from anyone else. But we never see each other except at camp."

Her mother studied the pictures in silence for a minute. "You miss your Sunnyside friends, don't you?"

"Yeah. A lot." With a sigh, Katie closed the album. "What's for supper?"

"Good grief, Katie! How can you possibly be hungry after that enormous dinner?"

"I'm not really hungry. I'm just bored." Gazing around her room, her eyes lit on her new board game. "Mom, you want to play Wacko with me?"

"I can't right now, dear. Your father and I have to go drop off some gifts at the nursing home where I've been volunteering. You can come with us if you'd like to."

As bored as Katie was, the thought of sitting around the nursing home wasn't exactly appealing. "No thanks."

"Why don't you ask Peter and Michael to play Wacko with you?"

Katie wrinkled her nose. "I'd have to be really desperate to do that."

12

Her mother threw up her hands. "Well, I've given you all the suggestions I can think of. Your father and I will be back in a few hours."

As soon as she left, Katie threw herself on her bed and stared up at the ceiling. Was this what it was going to be like every day for the next week? How was she going to stand it?

Maybe she should get involved in a big, fat book, something that would last a whole week. She got up, went to her bookcase, and looked over the possibilities. Nothing really attracted her, but she went ahead and selected a book.

But she was too restless to read. Finally, she put it back and headed downstairs to the basement.

Peter and Michael were still slamming the Ping-Pong ball across the table. Neither of them even glanced in her direction as she stood there watching them.

"Who's winning?" she asked.

Neither responded, but it wasn't necessary. The ball flew past Peter, and Michael tossed his paddle in the air. "One and one," he announced.

"I'll play the winner," Katie offered.

"Nah, I'm sick of this," Michael said. "Let's play that new Nintendo game." He was speaking to Peter, but then he smiled kindly at Katie. "You can play the Nintendo winner."

Katie made a face. "No thanks." She wasn't

crazy about Nintendo games, and she particularly didn't like playing them with either of the twins. They *always* won. And Katie didn't like playing games she didn't have a chance to win.

The boys ran upstairs, and Katie followed. For a moment, she watched while they set up the video game on the TV in the living room. It occurred to her that maybe there was something on TV to watch.

She went up to her parents' bedroom, flung herself on their bed, and picked up the remote control. The first thing she got on the screen were church services. She hit a button. Soap operas. Gross. She hit another one. This time she got a woman screaming in ecstasy because she'd just won a dumb washing machine.

She tried one more channel. The picture that appeared on the screen was in black and white. It looked like some old movie. She tried to watch, but she couldn't figure out what was going on. Still, she stared at the screen until her eyelids felt heavy. She closed them . . .

"Katie!"

She opened her eyes. Her parents were in the bedroom. And the TV screen displayed a news program. "Hi," she mumbled. "I guess I fell asleep." She wished she was still sleeping. "I was having such a nice dream. I was back at

Sunnyside, organizing a relay race in the swimming pool."

Her parents exchanged looks. "Well, I'm going to put some turkey sandwiches together for supper," Mrs. Dillon said. "How about giving me a hand?"

It was something to do. Katie dragged herself off the bed and headed down to the kitchen with her mother. While Mrs. Dillon began slicing turkey, Katie went to the refrigerator and pulled out lettuce, tomatoes, and a jar of mayonnaise.

"Katie, your father and I were talking . . . how would you like to have a party?"

"A party?" Katie looked at her mother in puzzlement. "How can I have a party? All my friends are out of town."

Her mother smiled. "What about bringing some friends *into* town?"

"What do you mean?"

"We thought you might like to have a house party."

"Mom, what are you talking about?"

Her mother's eyes sparkled. "A Camp Sunnyside reunion! Call all your friends from cabin six, and invite them here for a visit! They can come on Monday and stay until New Year's Day."

Katie was speechless. She stared at her

15

mother in disbelief. It took a full minute for her to absorb what her mother was saying. And then, she couldn't even respond properly. All she could do was jump up and down and shriek with joy.

❄ Chapter 2

The next morning, Katie hung up the phone and smiled in satisfaction. Two down, two to go. She placed a big red check mark next to Megan's name.

"Who's next?" her mother asked. She'd been standing by Katie's side, ready to take the phone and talk to each girl's mother or father after Katie issued the invitation.

Katie consulted her list. "I'm going to call Erin." Her expression must have changed because her mother asked, "What's the matter?"

"Oh, it would be just like Erin to mess this up. I'll bet she's got plans for the week."

Mrs. Dillon wasn't perturbed. "That's just one who might not be able to come. You've still got the others."

"But if it's going to be a real Sunnyside reunion, everyone has to be here," Katie insisted. "Even if Erin is a pain sometimes, I want her to come."

Her mother looked at her with concern. "But if she can't, she can't. Katie, everything can't always work out exactly the way you want it to."

"Yes, it can," Katie said with determination. "Nothing's going to ruin this reunion." She dialed Erin's number.

"Chapman residence," a voice announced.

That must be the maid, Katie thought. The Chapmans were rich—a fact Erin never let the others forget. "Can I speak to Erin, please?"

"Who may I say is calling?"

"Katie Dillon."

"One moment, please, and I'll see if she's available."

Katie rolled her eyes. Either Erin was there or she wasn't. What was this "available" business? She tapped her foot impatiently while she waited. And then she heard Erin's voice on the phone. "Hello?"

"Erin, this is Katie."

She knew she wouldn't hear the cry of pleasure she'd received from Sarah and Megan when she said that. And if Erin was surprised to hear from her, she certainly didn't sound like it. "Oh, hi, Katie."

Katie tried to sound just as casual as she explained why she was calling.

"You're having a reunion? Monday?" Erin's tone was disapproving. "That's not giving us much notice."

18

"Megan and Sarah can come."

"Well, they probably don't have anything else to do," Erin noted.

Katie's heart sank. "Do you?"

"There's a party at Alan's on Tuesday, and my friend Jessica's having a sleepover New Year's Eve."

Katie had expected something like this, and she was prepared to argue. But before she could begin, Erin continued.

"Actually, though, it might not be a bad idea to skip the party. Alan's been taking me for granted lately. It would really blow him away if I didn't show up."

Katie dimly remembered that Alan was Erin's sort-of boyfriend. She was the only girl in cabin six who had one. That was something else she wouldn't let the others forget.

"And I've been spending New Year's Eve at Jessica's forever. It's boring," she went on. "Yeah, I guess I can come. Let me ask my mother." A moment later, Mrs. Chapman came to the phone, and Katie handed it over to her mother.

When they finished talking, it was time for the last call, the most important one in Katie's opinion. Katie kept her fingers crossed while she hit the buttons.

There was no maid at the Sandburg resi-

19

dence. Trina herself answered the phone. "Hello?"

"Trina, it's Katie!"

Trina didn't squeal like Megan and Sarah had—that wasn't her style. But she certainly didn't sound bored like Erin. "Katie! How are you?"

"Great! And I'll feel even greater if you say yes."

"Yes to what?"

"My parents are letting me have a Sunnyside reunion this week! All the cabin six girls! Can you come?"

There was an audible gasp on the other end of the line. "This week?"

"Yeah! Megan and Sarah and Erin are coming Monday."

"Oh, Katie, this is perfect! My mother was just invited to go skiing with some friends. But she didn't want to leave me alone. And I didn't want to stay at my father's."

"Then you can come?"

"Hang on, let me ask my mother."

Within seconds, she was back. "I'll be there Monday!"

Katie let out a whoop. "Fantastic!"

As soon as she hung up, Katie raced into the kitchen. "They're coming!" she told her mother excitedly. "They're *all* coming! See, I told you everything would work out!"

"That's wonderful," Mrs. Dillon said.

The twins looked up from the kitchen table, where they were downing their third bowl of cereal. "How many girls are going to be here?" Peter asked.

"Four," Katie replied. "Five, counting me." She grinned wickedly. "You guys are going to be outnumbered for a change."

She was pleased to see the boys exchange looks of dismay.

"I have to get my room fixed up," Katie told her mother. "Where are the sleeping bags?"

"In the basement," Mrs. Dillon replied. "Let's see, you've got two beds in your room, so you'll need three bags. I hope there's enough room on your floor."

"There will be, as soon as I pick everything up," Katie assured her.

"Hey, I've got a better idea," Michael piped up. "Two of the girls can have our room."

"And where will you guys sleep?" Mrs. Dillon asked.

"Down the street, at Jimmy's," Peter said.

Mrs. Dillon shook her head. "Uh-uh. I'm not inflicting you two on Mrs. Hogan for a week."

21

"Besides," Katie said, "I *want* them all in my room. So it'll be just like cabin six." She hugged herself and danced around the room. "I can't believe they're going to be here Monday. I've got a lot to do."

Her mother nodded. "Like clean your room, I hope. And if we're going to have all that company, I'd better get to the supermarket."

"Want me to come with you?" Katie asked.

"No, you stay here and work on your room. Boys, help Katie bring the sleeping bags up from the basement."

"But we have to meet Jimmy," Michael protested.

"Yeah," Peter echoed. "Why do we have to help Katie? They're *her* guests."

"They're *our* guests," Mrs. Dillon corrected him. "And you have to help because I'm telling you to." Her tone confirmed this.

Katie shot the twins a smug look. Her heart swelled with triumph. For the next week, *they'd* be taking orders from her. Okay, maybe not directly from her, but through her mother. She had a pretty good feeling she could count on her parents to make the boys behave.

She ignored the moans and groans of the twins as they lugged the sleeping bags from the basement up to her room. "What a drag," Peter muttered. "Five girls."

22

"It might not be such a drag," Michael said. He nudged his brother. "Maybe we could have some fun with them."

Katie eyed him suspiciously. "What do you mean?"

Michael grinned. "You said you want it to be like camp, right? Maybe one of your friends will find a frog in her bed."

Now Peter was smirking too. "Yeah. Or maybe a snake."

Katie narrowed her eyes. "You wouldn't dare."

"Is that a challenge?" Michael asked. "Hey, Pete, you still got that Halloween costume? The monster one? Maybe you can pay the girls a midnight visit."

"You better not!" Katie exclaimed. "Listen, I'm serious. Megan scares easily."

"Oh really?" Peter cocked his head to one side. "That's *very* interesting."

Katie started to get nervous. "Look, you guys better stay out of our way. And if either of you hassles us . . ."

"Hassle you?" Michael snorted. "We just want to avoid you."

"That's fine with me," Katie replied. "And I'm sure my friends will be very grateful if you do."

They dumped the sleeping bags on her floor

and the boys left. Staring after them, Katie chewed on a fingernail. She was pretty sure they'd just been teasing her. But what if they *did* try pulling stupid stunts? Then she grinned. Just let them try. The Sunnyside girls could always strike back.

Anyway, she couldn't think about that now. She had some serious planning to do. She sat down at her desk, opened a notebook, and sharpened a pencil. Then she stuck the eraser end in her mouth and thought.

She needed to work out a schedule of activities. She had to come up with ideas, brilliant ideas, fabulous things for them all to do together. The girls would be counting on her to make this week fun. It was her responsibility, and not just because it was her home. Even back at Sunnyside, where they were given daily schedules, her cabin mates relied on her to figure out ways of making the good times even better.

If this Sunnyside reunion was going to be a success, it was up to her to make it one. She considered all the possibilities—outdoor activities, indoor activities, quiet times, silly times, wild and crazy times. As she thought, she jotted her ideas down.

Ice-skating, definitely. And cross-country skiing, if they could rent equipment. With a good snowfall, they could have a real snowball fight.

They could go to the movies one night. And she could get movie videos for those nights when they stayed in.

What else, she pondered. There was an indoor swimming pool at the Y. And bowling, that was a possibility. And board games, card games . . . they could put together that huge puzzle she'd gotten for Christmas. And of course they'd have to have a big celebration on New Year's Eve.

With a ruler, she drew lines on the paper, separating it into sections. She labeled each section with a day of the week. She divided each section for morning, afternoon, and night. Then she wrote in an activity for each time period.

It took ages. She kept changing her mind about the combinations, erasing, rewriting, crossing out. Finally satisfied, she recopied it all neatly. Then she ran downstairs.

Her mother was coming through the door gripping two large grocery bags. "Mom, take a look at this."

"How about giving me a hand with these first?"

"Sure." Katie grabbed a bag and set it on the kitchen table. "I guess you want me to help unpack and put everything away."

25

"That would be nice," her mother said. "Especially considering that most of this stuff is for your friends. Did you straighten up your room?"

"Uh, not yet. I was working on this." She waved the schedule at her mother. "Mom, I'll put this stuff away and clean my room. But would you look at this first?"

Mrs. Dillon took the sheet and examined it. "What *is* this?"

"A schedule for the reunion. I'm going to post it on my bulletin board, just like the schedules at Sunnyside. And all the girls will know what we're going to do every day."

She had anticipated praise for her efforts. What she didn't expect was for her mother to wrinkle her forehead and frown slightly.

"What's wrong with it?" Katie asked anxiously.

"Oh, nothing . . . but don't you think you'd better wait and find out what your friends *want* to do?"

"They'll want to do anything I suggest," Katie replied. "I *know* them. Oh, Mom, I'm so excited!" Impulsively, she threw her arms around her mother. "Thanks for letting me have this reunion. It's the best Christmas present ever!"

Mrs. Dillon stroked her hair. "I'm glad you're happy. Now, let's get this food put away."

Katie went to work emptying the bags. "Ooh, these are Sarah's favorite cookies! I wish it was summer, so we could have a cookout, like at camp."

"We could set up the grill on the screened-in porch," her mother suggested, "and pretend it's summer."

"That's a great idea!" Katie consulted her schedule. "I'll put it in here."

"Why don't we just wait and see when the girls *feel* like having a cookout?"

Katie shook her head. "I want everything organized. Just like at Sunnyside."

As soon as she finished helping her mother, she raced back upstairs to her room. It didn't take her too long to straighten it up. But the room needed more than neatening.

She took all her stuff off the bulletin board. Carefully, she centered the week's schedule and tacked it down. Then she pulled all the photos out of her album, and placed them all around the schedule.

Next, she dived under her bed and pulled out a long blue length of material.

"What's that?" Her father was peeking in.

"It's a Sunnyside banner. From one of our camp fires. Will you help me put it up?"

27

"Sure." Mr. Dillon grabbed one end. "Where do you want it?"

"On that wall," she said, handing him the thumbtacks. She was glad he hadn't asked how she'd acquired it. He probably wouldn't be very pleased to know that the cabin six girls had swiped it after lights out one night!

While her father tacked up the banner, Katie sat at her desk with a marking pen and a piece of cardboard. "This is for the door," she told her father, and displayed it to him.

"Cabin six," he read.

"So they'll know where they are," Katie said. She used a tack to stick it on her bedroom door.

She surveyed the room. It didn't look exactly like cabin six, but it was close. And then she had an inspiration.

She took the doll her grandmother had sent her down from the bookcase. Then she rummaged through a drawer for a Camp Sunnyside tee shirt and shorts. Within seconds, the doll was no longer in her velvet gown, looking elegant. She was a Sunnyside camper.

"Any other jobs I can do, ma'am?" her father asked.

Katie shook her head. "I think that's it for now. Thanks for putting the banner up, Dad.

I want everything to be perfect for the reunion."

Her father ruffled her hair. "I hope the week is everything you want it to be."

Katie knew it would be. How could anything go wrong? She was about to have Camp Sunnyside right here in her very own home!

Chapter 3

"Katie, your nose is going to become permanently stuck to that window."

Katie pulled back from the glass reluctantly and faced her mother. "What time is it?"

"About five minutes later than it was the last time you asked me."

Katie groaned. Every minute was beginning to feel like an hour.

"They'll get here," Mrs. Dillon assured her. "Why don't you busy yourself with something? You know, a watched pot never boils."

Katie groaned again. Her mother could be so corny. "Mom, don't say stuff like that in front of my friends, okay?"

"Stuff like what?"

"You know. A watched pot never boils. Haste makes waste. That kind of stuff."

Her mother eyed her quizzically. "Any other tips on how we should behave? I could pass them on to your father so he could watch what he says too. We wouldn't want to embarrass you in front of your friends."

Her mother could certainly be sarcastic. But Katie couldn't really blame her. "Sorry," she said. "I didn't mean to sound like that. I guess I'm nervous."

"Nervous? About what?"

"I don't know. I just want everything to be absolutely perfect this week."

Mrs. Dillon's expression softened. "I know. And I promise we'll all do everything we can to make sure your friends enjoy themselves."

"Thanks, Mom." Katie returned to her position at the window. Then she looked back. "Mom, there is one thing . . ."

"Yes?"

"Peter and Michael. Could you make them behave? Don't let them bug us, okay?"

"Don't worry about them," her mother stated. "The sight of all you girls will probably scare them away."

Katie wished she had a written guarantee of that. Then, the sound of a car pulled her face back to the window. "It's Trina!" she screamed. She tore out the front door.

"Katie! Your coat!" her mother yelled after her.

But Katie didn't feel the cold as she ran across the lawn toward the driveway. As soon as the car came to a stop, a figure leaped out of the passenger side and met her halfway. With a shriek, the girls threw their arms around each other and began jumping up and down.

Mrs. Dillon hurried up behind them. "Hello, Trina! Katie, you get right back into the house before you catch a cold." With a smile, she greeted Ms. Sandburg, Trina's mother.

Katie released Trina long enough for her friend to say good-bye to her mother. Then the girls ran into the house.

"Am I the first one here?" Trina asked, pulling off her coat.

"Yeah. Megan and Sarah are coming together," Katie told her. "Erin will probably come late, so she can make a grand entrance. Hey, where's your suitcase?"

Trina gasped. "My suitcase!"

"It's right here." Mrs. Dillon came in with the bag. "You left it in the car."

"Thank you," Trina said in relief. "Can you imagine if my mother had driven off with it?"

"I can't believe you left it in the car," Katie said. "That's not like you. You're the one at camp who always remembers what everyone else forgets!"

"I know." Trina sighed. "I've just been so spacey lately. My mother says it's typical pre-teenage behavior. But I'm starting to act like Megan!"

Mrs. Dillon took her coat. "Are you hungry, Trina? Would you like something to eat?"

"No, thank you," Trina replied. "We stopped for a hamburger on the way here."

"C'mon upstairs and see my room," Katie urged.

Trina gasped as she entered. "Katie! This is just like being back at camp!"

Katie nodded happily. "That's how I wanted it to look."

Trina wandered around. "This is so neat. I love the way you dressed up that doll! And the banner . . ."

Her words were music to Katie's ears. "I want this week to be just like we were all back at Sunnyside. Boy, do I miss that place. Don't you?"

"I haven't really thought about it that much," Trina replied. When Katie looked at her in surprise, she added, "I guess I've had so many other things on my mind."

"Like what?"

"Well, you know, home, my parents. It's been pretty weird."

Katie sat down on her bed. "Want to talk about it?"

Trina sounded hesitant. "Actually . . . no."

34

Katie understood that it was all painful for Trina. But she couldn't help feeling a little disappointed. She'd been looking forward to those intense, private conversations she and Trina used to have at Sunnyside. Of course, those talks were usually held after lights out, when everyone else was asleep. With the sunlight streaming in, the room didn't have the right atmosphere. Maybe later they could have a long heart-to-heart, and Katie could offer some good advice.

"Where's the rest of your family?" Trina asked.

"Dad's at work. And the twins are over at a friend's. I wish they'd stay there all week."

Trina grinned. "Now, Katie. They can't be that bad."

"Oh, yeah? You don't know them."

"I do sort of. I met them when they came to camp with your parents on Visitors' Day last summer."

Katie had completely forgotten that her brothers had been there. Looking back, she couldn't even visualize them at Sunnyside.

"I'll bet you're the only one who remembers they were there," she said. "If the others did, they probably wouldn't have agreed to come."

"I wish I had brothers or sisters," Trina said

35

in a wistful voice. She sat down on the bed next to Katie. "Being an only child isn't too great."

"*I* wouldn't mind," Katie said.

Trina went on as if she hadn't heard her. "It's a big responsibility. Everyone counts on you. Like, it's your job to make your parents happy."

Katie put an arm around her. "You can forget about that this week. Nobody expects you to do anything but have fun. Did you see our schedule?"

She pointed to the paper on the bulletin board. Trina went over and studied it. "Wow! We're going to do all this?"

"Yep! You wouldn't believe how hard I worked on it. Of course, Erin will probably find something to complain about. I'm counting on you to back me up."

There was a moment of silence before Trina said, "Yeah." Still looking at the schedule, she asked, "What movie are we going to see tonight?"

Katie hadn't put the title down because she wanted to announce it and see their expressions. "It's the new movie starring Rod Laney! I've been dying to see it, but I'm glad I didn't so we can all see it together!" In her mind she could see them all screaming at her favorite movie star when he appeared on the screen.

Then she realized Trina didn't look particularly excited by the notion. "What's the matter?"

"Oh, nothing. Well, it's just that I saw it last week back home."

"Oh, no!"

Quickly, Trina added, "But I wouldn't mind seeing it again."

"Good," Katie said in relief.

Trina wandered over to the window. "There's a car coming."

Katie joined her, and they watched as two girls got out. "It's Sarah and Megan!" Katie yelled. "Come on!"

They both ran downstairs, and entered the living room just as Mrs. Dillon was opening the door. For the next few moments, the house rang with shrieks and screams. In the midst of the commotion, Mrs. Dillon greeted them and collected coats. Katie directed them up to her room.

"I can't believe we're all here." Megan sighed in ecstasy.

"Sarah!" Trina exclaimed. "You changed your hair!"

"I had it layered and shaped. Do you like it?"

"Looks great," Trina replied. "Megan, I think you've grown."

"Half an inch," Megan said with pride.

Katie squinted. To her, Megan still looked

like a shrimp. "What have you guys been up to? I want to know *everything*. Sarah, you go first."

The girls gathered on her bed. "Well, I won an essay contest at school," Sarah said. "And we started a creative writing club."

"Are you going to write another romance book?" Katie asked. Sarah looked at her blankly. "Don't you remember?" Katie said. "Back at camp, when you started writing that romance about Carolyn and Teddy?"

"Oh, yeah. That was so dumb. Anyway, this creative writing club is neat."

"What kind of stuff are you writing?" Trina asked.

"Short stories and poems. It's not easy coming up with ideas. Our advisor says we should base stories on our own experiences."

"So I guess that's why you won't be writing romances." Katie chortled.

Sarah reddened slightly, and then she grinned. "Oh, you never know."

"Tell them," Megan urged.

"Tell us what?" Trina asked.

"Well, I sort of have a boyfriend," Sarah confessed.

Trina squealed, but Katie grimaced. This wasn't like Sarah. She'd never been boy crazy, like Erin.

"What's he like?" Trina asked, but before

Sarah could reply, Katie broke in. "What about you, Megan? What's going on?"

"I've been playing a lot of tennis," Megan said. "My instructor thinks I could go professional in a few years. He's been talking to my parents about sending me to a special tennis camp next summer."

Katie was shocked. "You can't do that! What about Sunnyside?"

Megan shrugged. "There's no real tennis program at Sunnyside."

Katie brushed that aside. "Oh, you can play plenty of tennis there. Besides, you couldn't survive a summer without us. You're such a total space cadet."

"I'm not that bad," Megan objected. "Okay, maybe I daydream a little—"

"A little!" Katie snorted.

"But not when I'm playing tennis," Megan said firmly. "Hey, is there an indoor tennis court in this town?"

Katie didn't know. Tennis wasn't her sport. It didn't matter, anyway. "You won't have time for tennis. Not with all the activities I've planned for us. But we've got a Ping-Pong table down in the rec room."

"Well, I guess that's better than nothing," Megan said.

"C'mon, I'll show you." Katie led them all

downstairs. In the living room, her mother was peering out the window.

"Good heavens, look at that."

"What?" Katie asked.

"A limousine. And it's turning into our driveway!"

The girls eyed each other knowingly. "Erin," they chorused. Joining Mrs. Dillon at the door, they all watched as a uniformed man stepped out of the long, black car and opened the back door.

"Is that a real fur coat she's wearing?" Sarah asked in wonderment.

"I'm sure she'll tell us if it is," Megan replied.

Erin's arrival was a bit more restrained than the others' had been. She wasn't the shrieking or hugging type. But even Erin, with all her sophistication, couldn't hide the fact that she was happy to see them.

Being Erin, her first comments were on their appearance. "Sarah, I like your hair. Megan, you're taller. Trina, you've lost weight." She shook her head with disapproval. "Katie, you look exactly the same." Then she turned to Mrs. Dillon.

"It's so lovely of you to have us all," she gushed. "And what a sweet house!"

Mrs. Dillon's eyes twinkled. "Why, thank you, dear."

"Come upstairs," Katie ordered.

Erin's eyebrows shot up when she saw Katie's bedroom. "Good grief. This looks like a Sunnyside cabin." That was basically what Trina had said, but Erin said it in an entirely different tone. "What's that? A *doll?!*" It was clear what she thought of that.

Katie wasn't insulted. This was basically what she expected from Erin.

"What's this?" Megan asked, looking at the bulletin board.

"It's our schedule of activities," Katie explained.

Sarah peered over Megan's shoulders. "Ice-skating?" she asked in dismay.

Erin joined her. *"Bowling?"*

"Gee, Katie, when are we supposed to *breathe?"* Megan asked. "It's not on the schedule."

Trina broke in. "C'mon, you guys, don't complain. Katie went to a lot of effort planning activities for us."

"That's right," Katie said gratefully. She knew Trina would back her up.

"And besides," Trina continued soothingly, "I'm sure she doesn't expect us to do *everything* on this schedule. It's just suggestions, right?"

Katie frowned, but she let that pass. She felt

41

sure that once they got into the swing of things, there wouldn't be any more complaints.

From downstairs came her mother's voice. "Girls! How about a snack?"

That suggestion received a lot more enthusiasm than Katie's schedule. They all raced downstairs and went into the kitchen. Katie noted with approval the sight of a freshly baked cake and a plate of brownies on the table. "It's like getting a goodie box from home at camp, right, guys?"

"Better," Megan said. "This stuff hasn't been sitting in a box for a week."

"I'm going to pick up your brothers," Mrs. Dillon told Katie. Katie made a face.

"Can't you just leave them wherever they are? Maybe they'll never find their way home."

Mrs. Dillon laughed as she walked out. Katie realized that Erin was looking at her with new interest. "I forgot about your brothers. They're thirteen, right?"

"Physically," Katie replied. "Mentally, they're about three. Believe me, Erin, even *you* wouldn't be interested in these boys. If you can call them boys. I think of them as something like insects."

Erin continued to look thoughtful, and it made Katie uncomfortable. She turned to Sarah. "Have you been doing anything besides reading and writing? Like, anything athletic?" She spoke teasingly, knowing full well that Sarah avoided sports like the plague.

"Believe it or not, I have," Sarah replied smugly. "We've got a new swimming pool at my school. And I've been taking diving lessons."

"Oh yeah?" Katie turned to her with a grin. "That's great. Think of how impressed Darrell will be next summer." Then she did what they always did when the handsome swimming coach's name was said. She put a hand over her heart and pretended to swoon.

No one seemed to notice. "Tell Erin about your boyfriend," Megan prompted.

"You've got a boyfriend?" Erin asked.

Before Sarah could get into that, Katie interrupted. "I wonder if Carolyn will be back at Sunnyside this summer."

"I wonder if I'll be back," Erin said. "My parents are talking about sending me to a camp abroad. France or Italy. Wouldn't that be neat?"

"My father wants me to go on a vacation with him out West next summer," Trina told them.

Katie gazed at them in horror. "Hey, you guys can't do that! That would only leave me and Sarah at Sunnyside!"

"Maybe not me," Sarah said. "I might apply for the summer honors program."

Katie was aghast. How could they all talk like

this, acting like they could just give up Sunny-side? It was a good thing she was having this reunion. After a week of reliving Sunnyside experiences together, they'd forget all these stupid ideas. She searched her brain for something to make them think about the good times.

"Hey, remember when we got to camp last summer and we found out about the boys from Camp Eagle coming?"

Megan nudged Sarah. "Speaking of boys . . ."

Sarah began telling them all about this boy she was hanging around with back home. Katie sank back in her chair and gritted her teeth. This was not exactly the type of conversation she'd expected to be hearing. She hadn't organized any activity for this afternoon, because she figured they'd want to sit around and reminisce about Sunnyside until dinner time. But no one was even talking about camp. She had to get this reunion going in the right direction.

As soon as there was a lull in the conversation, she jumped in. "Now that we're all here, you know what we should do? Sing the Sunnyside song."

Megan's forehead puckered. "Here?"

"It's a Sunnyside reunion, isn't it?"

Erin looked bored. "I don't even remember the words."

"Sure you do," Katie insisted. "Come on!" She

started them off. " 'I'm a Sunnyside girl, with a Sunnyside smile . . .' "

Erin groaned loudly, but Katie kept going. " 'And I spend my summers in Sunnyside style.' "

Megan, Sarah, and Trina finally joined in. " 'I have sunny, sunny days with my Sunnyside friends, And I know I'll be sad when the summer ends, But I'll always remember with joy and pride, My sunny, sunny days . . .' "

Their voices trailed off, leaving Katie alone to sing out the last two words, " 'at Sunnyside!' " She realized they were all looking at the doorway. Katie turned.

Peter and Michael were standing there. "Hey, don't quit now," Peter said. "That's a really awesome song."

"Yeah, very excellent," Michael added. "I heard it's going to be on Madonna's next album."

Katie glared at them furiously. Then she turned back to the others, to apologize for these creatures who happened to be her brothers.

To her surprise, none of the girls seemed particularly grossed out. Megan was eyeing the boys with undisguised interest. And Erin had on that awful icky smile she always wore when she confronted boys.

"Aren't you going to introduce us?" she asked Katie coyly.

"You know who they are," Katie replied. "They came to Visitors' Day last summer."

"But they might not remember our names," Trina reminded her gently.

"Yeah, where are your manners?" Peter asked Katie.

It took every ounce of Katie's willpower to keep from screaming for her mother to get rid of them. But she wanted to show the girls she could handle these bozos by herself. So she mumbled everyone's name. "Okay, I've introduced you. Now bug off, okay?"

When the twins finally left the kitchen, she said, "Don't worry about them. They're jerks."

"They don't seem so jerky to me," Sarah murmured.

"Me neither," Erin echoed.

Katie pretended not to hear that.

As they finished dinner that evening, Katie asked, "Dad, can you drive us to the movies tonight?"

"We're going to the movies?" Megan asked.

"Yeah. The new Rod Laney movie is playing."

"What are you boys up to this evening?" Mr. Dillon asked the twins.

46

"Jimmy and Al are coming over," Michael told them. "We're going to have a Nintendo competition."

"I always wanted to learn how to play those Nintendo games," Sarah said.

"They're great," Megan enthused. "I love Nintendo."

"You any good at it?" Peter asked her.

"Not bad," Megan said modestly.

The boys exchanged an unspoken message. Then Peter said, "You girls can play with us if you want."

"Great!" Megan exclaimed.

"I wouldn't mind doing that," Erin said.

"But we can't," Katie stated. "We're going to the movies."

Her mother spoke up. "Katie, maybe the girls are tired after their trips here. It might be a good idea to stay in tonight."

"We can always go to the movie another night," Trina said. "And I *am* kind of tired."

She had a point. Katie herself was a little tired after the day's excitement. But playing Nintendo with her brothers wasn't exactly what she considered a good substitute for the movie.

"Are you angry?" Trina whispered in her ear.

She always could read Katie's moods. Katie forced a smile. "No, it's okay. Like you said, we can go another night." It's really not okay, she

47

thought as she got up to clear the table. They hadn't even been here a day, and already the schedule was being changed.

But tomorrow will be different, she told herself. A fresh start. Maybe this day hadn't exactly lived up to her expectations, but there was a whole week ahead of them. Tomorrow would be the first real full day of the Sunnyside reunion. And Katie was going to make sure nothing kept it from being exactly the way she wanted it to be.

❄ **Chapter 4**

Katie was dreaming. In her dream, she was hiking through the Sunnyside woods, marching steadfastly forward, using a long stick to push twigs and stones out of her way. Behind her, the other cabin six girls were asking, "Where do we go now?"

"Follow me," Katie called. And they did.

Then the vision faded, and Katie was aware of the fact that she was lying down, not hiking. I'm in my top bunk in cabin six, she thought drowsily. I'll open my eyes as soon as Carolyn comes in and orders us up. That should be any minute now. . . .

But as her brain slowly came to life, she realized the sun wasn't streaming in and she couldn't hear the birds that gathered on the tree just outside the cabin windows. She opened her eyes. She was in her very own bedroom.

She'd had dreams like this a lot lately, and usually felt a wave of disappointment when she woke up. Not this time, though. She sat up and looked around happily from her position in the sleeping bag on the floor.

In the other sleeping bags, Megan and Sarah were still sleeping. Trina was in one of the twin beds. And in the other, Katie's own, was . . . Katie blinked. Where was Erin? The bed was empty.

Katie got up and grabbed her robe. She tried to move quietly so she wouldn't wake the others, but Trina stirred. "What are you doing?" she asked in a drowsy voice.

"I'm going to look for Erin," Katie whispered, and she slipped out the door. First, she peered down the hall at the bathroom, but the door was open and Erin obviously wasn't in there. An awful thought occurred to her. Could Erin have left? Had she decided this reunion wasn't such a great idea after all? Although she had certainly seemed to be having a good time last night playing Nintendo, Katie thought with a grimace. Still, it would be just like her to sneak out without even saying good-bye.

As she crept downstairs, she heard the twins' voices coming from the kitchen. And then she heard a familiar giggle. She went to the doorway.

Erin, fully dressed, was perched on the stool by the kitchen counter. Peter was leaning with his elbows on the opposite side of the counter, facing her. Michael was filling the blender, probably making one of his disgusting morning health shakes.

Katie said the first thing that came to her mind. "Erin, what are you doing in here?"

Erin gave her a look of wide-eyed innocence. "Is the kitchen off-limits?"

"No, of course not," Katie said quickly. "I was just surprised to see you up. You were never the first girl in the cabin to get out of bed."

Erin tossed her head. "We're not *in* the cabin, Katie. Anyway, I heard noises down here and they woke me up."

Funny, how the noises hadn't woken anyone else up, Katie thought. Of course, the girls always said Erin could hear boys a mile away. But why would she pull herself out of bed for *these* boys?

Katie fixed the boys with a stern look. "Could you guys keep it down from now on? I don't want you waking up my friends every morning."

"*I* didn't mind," Erin murmured.

"Good morning," Mrs. Dillon sang out as she sailed into the kitchen.

"Good morning," everyone chorused. "Where's Dad?" Peter asked.

51

"He's left already," Mrs. Dillon said. "He thought it would be best to shower, eat, and get out of the house before the campers take over the territory."

Katie eyed the twins meaningfully. She wished they'd take that notion to heart.

Her mother went to the refrigerator. "How do scrambled eggs sound to everyone?"

"Sounds great," Katie said. "Erin, let's go wake up the others."

Erin didn't budge. And Michael said, "Gee, Katie, I'll bet you could handle that job all on your own."

Katie considered sticking her tongue out at him but it wasn't worth the effort. She went out and ran upstairs.

Even though the door to the bathroom was closed, she could hear the noise inside it. They must all be brushing their teeth together, Katie thought. Just like they did at camp in the big cabin bathroom. Sure enough, the door opened and Megan, Sarah, and Trina came out.

"Morning," Katie called. "Mom's making scrambled eggs. I'll be down in a second." She went into the bathroom and took a quick shower. When she returned to the bedroom, she dressed hurriedly and headed back down to the kitchen.

Everyone was gathered around the kitchen table, digging into eggs and bacon and passing a pitcher of orange juice. With annoyance, Katie saw that Peter and Michael were still there. Not only that—they seemed to be monopolizing the conversation.

"It must be neat, having an identical twin," Megan was saying. "Do you guys ever fake people out, pretending one of you is the other one?"

"Sure," Michael said. "We do it all the time. It's our favorite trick."

"No one can tell us apart," Peter added.

"*I* can," Katie interjected.

"Like, what kind of tricks do you pull?" Sarah asked.

Peter and Michael grinned at each other, and then glanced at their mother.

"I'm going to take a shower," Mrs. Dillon said. As soon as she left the room, Peter started talking.

"Last year, Michael was having a rough time with math, and I hated language arts. So I took his math test, and he took my language arts."

Katie was shocked. "Boy, if Mom and Dad ever found out about that—"

"But they won't," Michael said. "Not unless a certain kid sister opens her big, fat mouth."

How dare he insult her like that in front of her friends? Katie thought furiously. Thank goodness, Trina jumped to her defense.

"Katie would never do anything like that."

Oh, wouldn't she? Katie thought. She filed this interesting bit of information away for future use.

"Another time," Peter continued, "I had this date for a dance at school. But at the last minute, this buddy of mine got tickets for a basketball game and invited me."

"So I went in his place," Michael finished. "And the girl never knew the difference!"

What a dumb story, Katie thought. But here were her cabin mates, all giggling. "Hurry up and eat," she told her friends. "We've got a lot to do today."

"What's on the schedule?" Trina asked.

"Ice-skating," Katie replied. She was pleased to see Megan's face light up.

"But I didn't bring my skates," Erin said. She gave the twins a flirtatious sidelong look. "Maybe I should just stick around here and—"

"You can rent skates at the lake," Katie broke in.

"Ice-skating," Sarah echoed. Her expression indicated that she wasn't exactly thrilled with that prospect. "I've never ice-skated before."

54

"Oh, it's easy," Katie assured her. "And it's a lot of fun. I'll teach you."

Sarah still looked uneasy. "I don't know. It's not something I ever really wanted to learn. And I don't have good balance. I've never even roller-skated."

Katie knew she had to be firm with her. Back at Sunnyside, Sarah wouldn't do anything athletic unless Katie pushed her. "You'll be fine," she stated in her best no-nonsense voice.

"What else are we doing today?" Megan asked.

"Tonight we're going bowling," Katie said.

Erin wrinkled her nose. "Why don't we go to that movie you were talking about last night?"

Katie shook her head. "I moved that to Wednesday."

"Jeez, Katie," Peter commented, "what is this, school or something?"

Katie ignored him. "You know," she said to the girls, "this is just like camp, all of us eating breakfast together."

"It's better than camp," Megan stated.

"Why?" Katie asked.

Megan reached for another helping of eggs. "The food!"

"And the company," Erin added, giving the twins another one of her silly corner-of-the-eye

55

looks. "I always wished Sunnyside would take boys."

"Yuck," Katie pronounced. "Okay, I don't mind having the Eagle boys there once in a while. But can you imagine what it would be like having boys there all the time?"

"I don't think it would be so bad," Megan commented. She turned to the twins. "Would you guys want to come to Camp Sunnyside?"

Michael grimaced. "We're too old for summer camp. That's kid stuff."

"I know what you mean," Erin said. "I think I'm getting too old for camp myself. Although a camp in France or Italy might not be so bad."

The direction of the conversation was bothering Katie. She had to get them all away from the boys. "C'mon, guys, hurry up. We want to get to the lake."

"Ice-skating on a lake," Trina murmured. "Katie, is that safe?"

Mrs. Dillon returned in time to hear her question. "It's not really a lake," she told Trina. "It's actually a rink, made to look like a lake."

"But I like to pretend it's a real lake," Katie said. "It feels nicer that way."

"Pretend?" Erin looked amused. "Honestly, Katie." Peter grinned, and Michael chortled.

Katie flushed. "I'm going to get my skates."

When she returned with them, the girls were gathered in the living room. "You guys ready? Let's go."

Peter and Michael walked in, both carrying their ice skates. Katie stared at them. "Where do you think you're going?"

Peter dangled his skates before her face. "We're not exactly playing golf with these."

Katie gritted her teeth. "You're not coming with us."

Michael looked at her smugly. "Oh, yeah? For your information, we were invited."

Katie whirled around. "Erin!"

"Don't blame her," Trina said hastily. "I invited them."

"You did?" Katie was aghast. How could Trina do that to her? And why would she want the boys with them anyway?

Sarah smiled shyly. "I invited them too."

Katie couldn't even respond. Had they all lost their minds?

"C'mon, let's go," Michael said. Katie didn't like the way they all started moving in response. Okay, maybe they were all just trying to be polite. But this was too much.

Her mood improved when they stepped outside. It was a gorgeous winter day, cold, but without a biting wind. And the sun was shining brightly. Katie lagged behind the others with Megan. "It's a great day for ice-skating."

Megan agreed. "Absolutely perfect."

"I'm not so sure of *that,*" Katie replied. "It would only be perfect if *they* weren't here." She indicated her brothers ahead.

"Oh, I think they're funny," Megan argued. "You just can't see what's good about them because they're your brothers."

Katie sniffed. "Hah! They could be total strangers and I wouldn't like them."

Megan grinned. "If they were total strangers, you wouldn't *know* them!"

Katie had to laugh. And she decided to look on the bright side. It was a great day. She had her friends around her. She wasn't going to let her brothers bother her.

It was early enough that the lake wasn't too crowded with skaters. Katie led the girls to the booth where they could rent their skates. But when Sarah requested her size, the man shook his head. "I don't have any size three's left."

Relief flooded Sarah's face. "That's okay. I'll just watch."

But Katie wasn't going to let her off that easy. "Get the next size."

"But they'll be too big," Sarah protested.

"The laces will hold them on," Katie assured

her. Sarah looked doubtful, but she accepted the next larger size from the man.

Katie went to a bench with the others to put on her skates. Then she stepped onto the ice. "Let's have a race," she called out.

"Okay," Peter said. Katie changed her mind. If the boys raced with them, they'd win. Besides, Trina and Megan had already started off, skating slowly across the ice. Katie took off after them. As she approached, she did a turn, and saw Sarah still standing uncertainly on the edge. She was eyeing the ice as if she expected it to open up and swallow her.

Poor Sarah, Katie thought. She needs me. She started back toward her. But just as she was almost at the edge, Michael zoomed in front of her. "Would you like me to take you out on the ice?" he offered Sarah.

Sarah looked enormously grateful. She took Michael's arm, and made a few tentative steps.

Katie watched for a minute, to make sure Michael wasn't going to do one of his typically obnoxious stunts, like send Sarah flying onto the ice. But he seemed to be really trying to help her.

Still, she had to get them to stop interfering with her reunion. Looking across the lake, she saw Erin skating with Peter. Katie sighed.

Maybe tonight, after lights out, she'd have a good heart-to-heart with the girls.

She skated off and joined Trina and Megan.

"This is so nice," Trina said. "Katie, thanks so much for inviting us here. I really needed to get away from home."

Katie wanted to hug her, but she was afraid they'd both lose their balance. "I'm so glad you're having a good time."

"Yeah, it's great being here," Megan said. "Trina, it must be really tough for you with your parents being divorced."

Trina nodded. "I feel like I'm caught in the middle. My mother will want me to do something with her, and my father will call and want me to go someplace with him. And I don't want to hurt either of them. It's not easy being the only child. You don't know how lucky you are, Katie."

"No, I certainly don't," Katie agreed. "If you had to live with two inconsiderate brothers, you wouldn't know you were lucky either."

"Here comes one of them now," Megan said. Katie turned and saw Michael approaching.

"See what I mean?" she told them. "He's supposed to be helping Sarah, and he's just deserted her."

Michael skidded to a stop in front of them. "I

don't think your friend should be on the ice," he told Katie.

"Why?"

"Because she can't balance herself, especially with skates that are too big."

"She's just not trying," Katie said. "You have to push her to work at it."

"If she doesn't want to skate, she shouldn't *have* to skate," Michael argued. "Why don't you just let her be?"

"I know her better than you do," Katie shot back. "You just don't really want to help her, that's all." She left her brother and skated over to the edge of the ice where Sarah stood.

"What's the matter?" Katie asked.

Sarah raised a woebegone face. "Katie, I don't think this is my sport."

Katie dismissed that. "That's what you said about swimming back at Sunnyside last summer."

"I mean it this time," Sarah insisted. "I don't feel comfortable doing this. I think I'll just go sit on that bench and watch you guys."

"Don't be silly," Katie said briskly. "C'mon, I'll help you."

"I really don't want to do this," Sarah pleaded, but Katie grabbed her arm and led her forward.

"Just put one foot in front of the other and glide." Gingerly, Sarah inched forward.

"Come on, don't be so scared," Katie urged, giving her a slight push. It was a mistake. Sarah's feet flew out from under her. She flailed her arms and came down on her hand, hard.

Horrified, Katie stared at the crumpled figure on the ice. Behind her, Michael, Megan, and Trina appeared. "Are you okay?" Trina cried out.

Michael knelt down on the ice next to Sarah. Slowly, Sarah pulled herself up, putting pressure on one hand to do it. "Ow!" she screamed.

"What is it?" Katie asked frantically.

"She hurt her hand," Michael said.

Pain creased Sarah's face. "I think it's my wrist," she moaned.

Peter and Erin skated over to them. "What's going on?" Erin asked.

"Sarah fell and hurt her wrist," Michael said. "It could be broken."

Katie heard Trina murmur, "Oh, no!" And she noticed with alarm that Sarah was getting awfully white.

"I guess I better go call my mother," Katie said.

Michael shook his head. "She was getting ready to go out when we left. Besides, the hospital's only a block away. Peter and I will take her to the emergency room. Sarah, do you think you can walk?"

He took hold of her arm and helped her up. Peter went to her other side and together the boys led her off the ice. Megan and Trina followed them, and started unlacing Sarah's skates. Erin stroked Sarah's head and spoke comfortingly.

Katie hurried over there too. "I'll go with you to the hospital."

"No, you stay here with your friends." Michael spoke with authority. "Maybe you better take them on home. We'll call you there after the doctor looks at her."

"They're good at taking charge, aren't they?" Megan whispered in admiration.

Katie nodded reluctantly. They certainly were taking charge. But that was supposed to be *her* job.

"Sarah, would you like some tea or hot chocolate?" Mrs. Dillon asked anxiously.

Curled up on the couch, Sarah nodded weakly. "If it's not too much trouble. Hot chocolate would be nice."

"Are you sure the doctor said it's just a sprain?" Megan asked. "You look really pale."

"It hurts a lot," Sarah whispered, gazing at the wrist wrapped in an elastic bandage.

63

"Did you take the pills for the pain?" Peter asked. When Sarah nodded, he said, "They should start working soon."

"What are you, a doctor?" Katie asked.

"Now, Katie," Mrs. Dillon said, coming back in the living room with a tray in her hands. "I think the boys handled this very well."

"They really did," Erin said, looking at the boys in a positively worshipful way. "I don't know what we would have done without them."

I could have handled it, Katie thought, if someone had given me a chance.

"Sarah, did you call your father?" Mrs. Dillon asked.

"The doctor at the hospital called him. He said he'd come get me if I wanted to go home. But the doctor said I should feel better tomorrow, so I told my father I'll wait till then and see if it still hurts."

"We'd like you to stay," Mrs. Dillon said. "What else did the doctor say?"

"Just to keep the bandage on."

"And she's not supposed to use that hand," Michael added.

"We'll make sure she's properly waited on," their mother said. "Now, I'll go fix some hot chocolate for the rest of you." She went back to the kitchen.

"I guess that means no bowling tonight," Katie said.

"Katie!" Trina gazed at her reproachfully. "How can you be thinking about bowling now after what happened to Sarah!"

"Yeah," Peter chimed in. "Especially when you were the one responsible."

"That's not true!" Katie exclaimed.

"I saw you push her," Peter stated.

She couldn't deny that. "Okay, maybe it is a little true. But I didn't mean it!"

"I know you didn't mean it," Sarah said. "It's not your fault. I'm just clumsy."

Katie felt awful. "I'm sorry, Sarah!"

Sarah smiled. Her eyes were getting glazed. Katie figured that must be the effect of the pain-killers.

"Maybe we should get a video for tonight," Megan suggested.

Katie considered this. She had videos down on the schedule for Thursday night. But maybe by then they could go bowling. Even if Sarah couldn't play, she could keep score. "Okay. There's a video store just a few blocks from here. Who wants to go with me?"

But everyone was crowding around Mrs. Dillon, who had just returned with the hot chocolate and a tray of brownies.

"I guess I could go by myself," Katie mur-

65

mured. Luckily, Trina picked up on the reluctant tone in her voice.

"I'll go with you," she said. The girls got their coats and headed out.

"I really didn't mean to hurt Sarah," Katie said as they walked to the video store.

"I know you didn't," Trina said. "And I didn't mean to scold you before. It's just that you sounded more interested in keeping to your schedule than you were in Sarah."

"I was just thinking out loud," Katie told her. "I mean, I'm responsible for the reunion. I have to make sure everyone has a good time."

"Don't worry about it so much. We can all come up with good ideas for things to do."

Privately, Katie wasn't so sure of that. She couldn't remember any of them coming up with too many great ideas back at Sunnyside. Okay, once in a while, maybe. But in all modesty, she knew she was the bright-idea one.

"Of course, they have to be activities Sarah can participate in," Trina continued.

"I'll work on the schedule when we get home," Katie replied. They entered the video store and started looking around at the films that were displayed.

"What kind of movie should we get?" Trina asked.

Katie grinned. Trina was proving her point.

She *was* the one everyone turned to for decisions.

"Nothing scary," she said. "Megan gets freaked out. Remember that time at camp, when we saw that movie about the teenager who was really a witch? That's what made Megan decide that day camper was a witch."

"Oh, yeah. Okay, nothing scary."

"And I don't want any really mushy love stories," Katie continued. "They always make Erin start acting goofy. And no adventure movies either. If we show one of those, the twins will want to watch."

"What about something animated?" Trina asked.

Katie shook her head. "Sarah doesn't like cartoons. I think we should get a comedy." They went over to that section of the store, and perused the selections.

"Ooh, here's one with Rod Laney in it," Katie said, grabbing the box.

"I've seen that one," Trina said. "I'll bet everyone else has too."

"Yeah, but a Rod Laney movie you can see over and over," Katie decided. "And I know Sarah likes him. Let's get it."

"Okay," Trina agreed. They went to the counter to rent the film.

"I want dinner to be special for Sarah," Katie

said. "I'm trying to remember. What's her favorite food?"

Trina thought about that. "I think she likes just about anything."

"Mom said we can order in take-out food tonight," Katie told her. "We've got lots of possibilities. There's pizza, Mexican food, Chinese food—"

"Sarah told me once she loves Chinese food," Trina said.

"Then that's what we'll get," Katie decided. She started feeling a lot better, knowing she had the whole evening planned. Chinese food and a Rod Laney movie. It would help make up for what she'd done to Sarah, and everyone else would enjoy them too.

Not to mention the fact that the twins didn't like Chinese food. And they *hated* Rod Laney.

"It's so nice not having to cook tonight," Mrs. Dillon said in a pleased voice. They were all gathered in the living room. Sarah was still on the couch, but she was sitting up and her face had some color. Mr. Dillon was glancing through the newspaper, and Megan lay sprawled on the floor with another section of it.

"Where are Peter and Michael?" Erin asked casually, as she applied another coat of polish to her nails.

"Playing Ping-Pong downstairs," Katie said. She hoped it would prove to be an all-night tournament.

"I'm getting hungry," Mr. Dillon said. "What should we order?"

"Chinese food," Katie said promptly. She was surprised to see Sarah wrinkle her nose. "I thought you liked Chinese food."

"I do," Sarah said. "But my father was out of town for a few days last week, and my sister and I ordered Chinese food almost every night."

Just then Peter and Michael walked in. "What's for dinner?"

"We're ordering out," Mrs. Dillon said. "Katie just suggested Chinese food."

"Gross," Peter said. "What about pizza?"

Sarah brightened. "That sounds great."

"Yeah," Megan echoed. "I vote for pizza!"

"Sounds like pizza has the vote," Mr. Dillon said. "Now, what about toppings? Pepperoni? Mushrooms?"

Katie frowned. It wasn't that she didn't like pizza. But once again, the twins were taking over. At least she already had the video for tonight. They couldn't do anything about that.

"Oh, wow!" Megan yelled.

"What?" Trina asked.

"Guess what's on TV tonight? *It's a Wonderful Life!*"

"Oh, my," Mrs. Dillon said, smiling. "That's such a beautiful film."

"What's it about?" Trina asked.

"It's so neat," Megan said enthusiastically. "It's about this man who has all these bad things happen to him. And he wishes he'd never been born. So this angel comes and shows him what life would have been like for everyone he knows if he hadn't been born." She paused. "I don't want to tell you any more. It would spoil it."

"I've heard of that movie," Sarah said. "It's one of my dad's favorites. I've always wanted to see it."

"You'll have your chance tonight," Megan said.

"Sounds good to me," Erin commented.

"But I got us a video," Katie protested. "Rod Laney, in *Happy Holidays.*"

"I've seen that twice," Erin said.

"And it wasn't even all that funny," Megan said. "Let's watch *It's a Wonderful Life.*"

Heads were bobbing. And then they all resumed their discussion of pizza toppings.

Katie leaned back in her chair. She couldn't help feeling a little disappointed. But she wasn't going to fuss, she decided in resignation. She'd eat pizza. She'd watch *It's a Wonderful Life.* She'd try as hard as she could to be a good sport.

But it was starting to seem like all her careful planning was for nothing.

Chapter 5

"I could see that movie a hundred times," Megan announced as she helped Katie load the dishwasher with the breakfast dishes. "I loved when he was seeing all those old friends and they didn't know who he was. Not even his own mother knew him! It was amazing."

"That's because he never existed," Trina noted, scraping leftovers into the garbage can. "Everything was different because he never lived."

Sarah, using only her left hand, carried some dishes to the sink. "Like his younger brother being dead, because he hadn't been there to save him from drowning. That was enough to make his life worthwhile."

Erin sat at the counter, watching the others work. "And his wife never married because he was the only man she could have ever loved. That was so sad."

"But it was nice the way he found out he was

more important than he thought he was," Trina said. "It was wonderful at the end."

"I love happy endings in movies," Megan agreed. "But even though everything worked out, I cried."

"We all did," Sarah said. "Except Katie."

"Katie, didn't you like the movie?" Trina asked.

Katie managed to squeeze one more glass into the dishwasher rack. "It was okay, I guess. But it was kind of old-fashioned. I like modern movies, where things happen that could really happen."

"It seemed pretty real to me," Megan said. "I believed everything that happened."

Katie snorted. "That's just because you've got a wild imagination. Honestly, Megan, you don't really believe an angel can come and grant your wishes, do you?"

"You never know," Megan replied. "Just because it never happened to you doesn't mean it couldn't happen."

"It's funny," Sarah said thoughtfully. "At home, whenever I say 'I wish I could do this,' or 'I wish I had that,' my father always says, 'Be careful what you wish for, because you might get it.' I never understood exactly what he meant. But after seeing that movie, I think I do.

I mean, you could get something you wish for, and then be sorry you ever wished for it."

Katie rolled her eyes. That didn't make any sense to her at all. If she got something she wished for, she'd never be sorry she got it. "Well, I still like real-life movies better. Like the one we're going to see today."

"Are we going to the movies today?" Erin asked.

"Yeah, remember? The new Rod Laney movie." Didn't they ever look at the schedule? she wondered. Of course, it was pretty messy now, with all the changes she'd had to make. But after all the work she'd put into it, the least they could do was glance at it once in a while.

"Where did Peter and Michael run off to this morning?" Erin asked.

"I don't know and I don't care," Katie replied.

Her mother walked in. "Oh, girls, how nice of you to clean up the kitchen! Sarah, how's your hand feeling?"

"Much better," Sarah said. "It only aches a little when I use it."

"You won't need to use it today," Katie said. "Mom, can you take us to the movie theater at the mall?"

"I think that can be arranged," Mrs. Dillon said. "What time is the movie?"

Katie had checked that the day before. "Two

o'clock." She did some mental calculations. "We want to get there at one, so we can eat lunch at the new taco place. So we should leave here at twelve forty-five." She glanced at the clock. "It's ten o'clock now. That gives us two hours and forty-five minutes to put together the puzzle."

"What puzzle?" Megan asked.

"The one I got for Christmas. It's on the schedule for this morning," she added pointedly.

"Oh, how fantastic!" Trina exclaimed. But it only took a second for Katie to see she wasn't referring to the puzzle. Trina was looking at a calendar on the wall.

"What's fantastic? A calendar?" Katie asked.

"The pictures," Trina replied. She lifted the calendar pages and exposed the various pictures of flowers. "These are beautiful. Where did you get this, Mrs. Dillon?"

"At the museum right here in town," Mrs. Dillon said. "Those are pictures of some of the paintings there."

Sarah turned to her. "Mrs. Dillon, is there a public library around here?"

"Of course, dear. In fact, it's quite a nice one for a town this size."

"Do you think we could stop there on the way to the mall?" Sarah asked. "I forgot to bring a book with me, and I need something to read."

76

Katie thought about their schedule. "You don't have any time to read this week." She felt, rather than saw, her mother's reproving look.

"Katie, there's always time to read. Of course we can stop at the library, Sarah. Katie can use her card to check a book out for you. We should leave around noon then, to give you some browsing time."

That would leave only two hours for the puzzle, Katie thought. But she couldn't bring herself to point that out to Sarah. She still felt a little guilty about Sarah's fall on the ice. If stopping at the library was what Sarah really wanted to do, Katie would go along with it.

"You know, the museum I mentioned is right next door to the library," her mother added. "Trina, would you like to see the real paintings of those flowers?"

Trina clapped her hands together. "I'd love that! Can we go there?"

"I don't see why not," Mrs. Dillon said. "But we'd better leave around eleven then, if you want to make that movie. And *I'd* better get dressed," she added as she left the kitchen.

Katie frowned. "There's no way we can do that puzzle in an hour."

"Could we do it tonight?" Trina asked. "I'd really like to see these paintings."

"Well, I'd planned that we'd play Wacko tonight," Katie began, and then she stopped. Maybe she *was* being a little silly. "Oh, sure, I guess that's okay."

"I've never been to a real museum," Megan said. "This is neat."

Katie'd been to the museum before, and she had to admit she'd enjoyed the visits. She just wished *she'd* been the one to suggest it.

"I'm glad Sarah's getting to come here," Trina said to Katie as they all walked up to the library.

Katie nodded. "Yeah, but I hope she doesn't plan on spending the rest of the week reading."

"Well, if anyone can pull her away from her books, it's you," Trina noted.

Katie smiled modestly. At least Trina was admitting that Katie *did* have some influence around here.

"I don't see why we *all* had to come to the library," Erin complained.

"Erin, this is a Sunnyside reunion," Katie explained for what felt like the zillionth time. "We do everything together at Sunnyside, right? So we're doing everything together here, too."

Erin didn't seem very satisfied with that answer. But at least Sarah looked ecstatic as they entered the library. She headed directly to the young adult fiction section, and was soon engrossed in her browsing. Trina and Megan were looking at books too, while Mrs. Dillon perused the best-seller display.

Katie followed Erin to the magazine rack. "Will your brothers be home tonight?" Erin asked Katie.

It was impossible for Katie to keep the annoyance out of her voice. "Why do you care? Look, Erin, I don't want them hanging around with us. We're supposed to be having fun."

Her testy tone didn't bother Erin. "Maybe having boys hang around is my idea of fun." She picked up a teenage magazine and began flipping through it. "Ooh, look at this." She pointed to a model wearing a sequined sweater. "This is just the kind of sweater I've been wanting. But I haven't seen anything like it in the stores back home."

Katie glanced at it. "It's okay."

"And I like this hairstyle, too," Erin went on. "I need a haircut. Katie, are there any good beauty salons in this town?"

"Erin, we don't want to spend an afternoon watching you get your hair cut."

"You don't have to," Erin replied coolly. "I could go by myself."

Katie pressed her lips together tightly. Erin just absolutely refused to get into the spirit of the reunion.

Sarah took an awfully long time choosing her books, and they ended up spending more time there than Katie expected. Katie thought of how Carolyn always kept them right on schedule at Sunnyside. What they really needed here at the reunion was a counselor.

At the museum next door, they joined a group listening to a woman describe each painting and telling them about the artist who painted it. Katie kept looking at her watch. The woman spent ten minutes on one painting alone! And when they finished with the tour, Trina spent fifteen minutes in line at the gift shop to buy a calendar. At this rate, they'd never get to the mall.

When Mrs. Dillon finally dropped them off there, it was one-thirty. "We're going to have to eat fast," Katie told the others. "The movie's at two."

But Erin didn't appear to be in any hurry. She just stood there, looking around. "Katie, you've got some great stores here," she said, her eyes gleaming as she took in the sights. "This is better than the mall back home."

"Well, you don't have time to go inside them now," Katie stated firmly.

Erin's attention was diverted, but not because of Katie's comment. It was a result of Megan's sudden cry.

"Katie, there's your brothers!"

Katie turned. Sure enough, Peter and Michael, carrying tennis rackets, were coming out of a sporting goods store. Unfortunately, Megan's shrill voice had carried. The boys waved and ambled toward them.

"Hi!" Erin called. "What a coincidence!" She cocked her head coyly. "Did you two *know* we were coming out here?"

The boys shook their heads. "Nah," Peter said. "It's just your lucky day, I guess." Erin giggled.

They really were awful, Katie thought. "What are you guys doing here?" she demanded.

"I had to get my racket restrung," Michael said.

Peter demonstrated a swing, which almost hit Katie in the head. "We're playing this afternoon."

Megan acted like she'd just been hit by a lightning bolt. "You are? Is there an indoor tennis court around here? Katie, you didn't tell me about that!"

"You want to come play?" Michael asked.

"She can't," Katie interjected. "We're all going to the movies."

"But I'd rather play tennis," Megan said plaintively.

"You don't have a racket," Katie pointed out.

"They've got extras at the court," Peter said. "We'll get one for you."

"Terrific!" Megan squealed, hopping up and down.

Katie didn't know who to be furious at—Megan or the twins. Knowing Megan's passion for tennis, she couldn't really blame her for wanting to play. It was much easier to blame those wretched, disgusting brothers of hers for bringing the subject up. But she didn't want to create a scene in front of her friends.

"Do what you want," she muttered to Megan. At least she had the satisfaction of seeing Erin's disappointed face as Megan took off with the twins.

Then she looked at her watch and groaned. "It's ten till two! We're not going to have time to eat. We have to get to the theater immediately."

"But I'm starving," Sarah wailed.

And then Erin gasped. "Look! In that window!"

"What?" Katie asked.

"It's that sweater I saw in the magazine! The one I've been wanting!" She started walking toward the store. Katie ran after her, and the others followed.

"We don't have time, Erin! Look, we'll go by there after the movie, okay?"

"But it might be gone by then!" Erin argued. "I absolutely *have* to get that sweater!"

"I've got an idea," Trina said. "Sarah's hungry and Erin wants to shop. I'm hungry too, and I wouldn't mind looking at some clothes. So why don't we eat and shop instead of going to the movie this afternoon? We can always go to see the movie tonight or tomorrow."

"Sounds good to me," Erin said.

"Perfect," Sarah piped up.

Katie was bewildered. Since when did Trina make the plans for cabin six? What was going on here? And no one was even waiting for her approval! Already, they were all moving toward the store where Erin saw the sweater.

At least Trina had the courtesy to turn and beckon to her. "C'mon, Katie!"

What could she do? Her shoulders slumped, Katie slowly followed.

Katie stood alone in her bedroom and examined the schedule on the bulletin board. With all the cross outs and erasures, it wasn't easy to read, but it wasn't difficult to see that the girls were completely off schedule. Here she'd put so much time and thought into creating this plan, and her friends were totally ignoring it.

She couldn't understand. This never happened at Sunnyside. Okay, sometimes when it rained, the schedule was scrapped. But normally, they followed it right down the line.

And it wasn't just the schedule that was bothering her. Nothing seemed right at all. She'd expected this reunion to be just like being at Sunnyside. She'd assumed the girls would act like they did at camp. She thought they'd follow her lead, listen to her ideas, and respond with enthusiasm. Why was everything so different here?

It's Peter and Michael, she decided. They're the ones who are messing everything up. Well, she wasn't going to let this continue. This was Wednesday. There was still lots of time before the girls had to go home.

"Katie! Dinner!" It was the second time her mother had called her to come down. With a new resolve, Katie left her room and ran downstairs.

Everyone was gathered at the table. As her mother passed the platter of chicken, Mr. Dillon asked, "What did you girls do today?"

"We went to the library," Sarah said.

"And the museum," Trina added.

"I played tennis," Megan announced.

"No kidding," Peter said. "She really slaughtered me, too."

Despite her feelings, Katie couldn't help smirking.

"You probably just had a bad day," Erin assured him.

"How was the movie?" Mrs. Dillon asked.

"We didn't go," Katie said. "We're going tonight."

"What are you going to see?" Michael asked.

"The new Rod Laney movie."

Michael responded by making a gagging sound.

"Not at the table, Michael," Mrs. Dillon said mildly.

"We don't have to see that one," Erin said. "Maybe we could go see something else."

"No!" The sound of her own outburst startled Katie. Quickly, she tried to make up for it. "I mean, that's what we all want to see, right?"

Thank goodness, Trina didn't let her down. "Sure, I wouldn't mind seeing it."

"It's okay with me," Sarah said, and Megan nodded.

"What time is the movie?" Mr. Dillon asked.

"I'll look in the paper," Katie said. She ran out to the living room, rifled through the newspaper, and brought the entertainment section back to the table. Opening it to the movie page, she ran her finger down the listings. "Oh, no."

"What's the matter?" Sarah asked.

"It's not playing anymore," Katie replied miserably.

Peter leaned over to look at the paper. "Hey,

Midnight Menace is playing. I've been wanting to see that. Some guys at school said it was outrageous."

"Yeah," Michael said. "I heard it's excellent."

"Why don't we all go see that?" Erin suggested.

Katie shook her head. "No, not that one." And that wasn't just because she didn't want her brothers going to the movies with them. *Midnight Menace* sounded like a scary movie to her. Even though she enjoyed scary movies, she knew how they freaked Megan out.

"Why not?" Erin asked. "It sounds cool."

Katie looked at Erin, then at Megan, then back at Erin again. But Erin didn't get the message.

"Here's a comedy," Katie said. *"Family of Fools.* How about that?"

"I've seen it," Sarah replied. "It was dumb. Let's go see that menace movie."

Katie looked at her in surprise. She thought Sarah would be more sensitive to Megan's fears. And she was even more surprised when Megan said, "Yeah, that sounds neat."

"Sounds like *Midnight Menace* wins," Michael said, shooting a smug look at Katie. Katie didn't know what to say. She concentrated on her food, and barely spoke for the rest of the meal.

But later, when they were clearing the table, she pulled Megan aside. "Are you sure you want to see that movie? I think it's supposed to be scary."

"I don't mind," Megan said.

Katie looked at her closely. And then she figured out what was going on. Megan was trying to be brave, she decided. She didn't want the others to know how truly frightened she was at the thought of seeing a scary movie.

But Katie remembered the night they all saw a scary movie at Sunnyside. And Megan woke up with nightmares in the middle of the night. Katie had been the one who sat on the bed with her until she calmed down.

The same thing will probably happen tonight, Katie thought. But at least she'd be there to comfort Megan. And she had to admit, the thought wasn't that unappealing. It made her feel important, knowing that Megan would need her that night.

Later, sitting in the dark theater, Katie decided she'd better prepare herself for a major middle-of-the-night crisis. *Midnight Menace* was more than just a little scary. It was downright horrifying.

It was about a man who seemed perfectly normal during the day. But every night, at midnight, he turned into the most frightening creature Katie had ever seen in a movie. He roamed through the town terrifying people and doing things that made Katie's stomach turn over. The screams that echoed in the theater let her know she wasn't alone.

She'd always considered herself a pro when it came to horror movies. But this one had her putting her hands over her eyes. Every now and then, she sneaked a peek at Megan. At least she hadn't run out of the theater. But Katie knew they'd both have a sleepless night. Megan was going to need her.

When the movie was over, the group drifted outside to wait for Mr. Dillon, who was picking them up.

"That was great," Peter enthused.

Erin agreed. "But it was so creepy! I don't know what I would have done if you guys hadn't been there."

"Megan," Katie whispered, "how do you feel?"

"Fine," Megan replied. "Why?"

Katie smiled kindly. "Well, that was a pretty scary movie. Worse than the one we saw at Sunnyside that time. Remember?"

"Oh, right." Megan grinned at Katie. "But I'm not scared of horror movies anymore. I've been to lots of them back home, and I didn't have any nightmares."

"You didn't?"

Megan shook her head proudly. "I guess I grew out of that."

"Oh. Well, that's good."

But as they waited for Mr. Dillon, Katie was confused. She really *was* glad that Megan wasn't having nightmares anymore. But at the same time, she was strangely disappointed.

❄ Chapter 6

Katie was dreaming again. And like in her last dream, she was back at Sunnyside. Only this time, she wasn't hiking through the woods. She was in cabin six, standing by the bulletin board where the daily schedule was posted.

"It's time to go to the pool," she was announcing to her cabin mates. "We've got free swim today. Let's challenge cabin seven to a water volleyball game."

A babble of voices greeted this suggestion. They seemed to all be speaking at once, but Katie could hear each comment distinctly.

"No, I'm going to arts and crafts," was Trina's response.

"I'm playing tennis," Megan announced.

"I'm doing my nails," Erin said.

"And I'm going to read," stated Sarah.

"But you can't!" Katie protested. "We have to go to the pool! It says so right here!"

"So what?"

"Who cares?"

"Big deal!"

"We don't have to listen to *you!*"

The voices went on like that, but they merged and blended until they became one big noise. And soon they didn't even sound like voices anymore, but like a low roar punctuated by banging sounds.

Katie woke up in a cold sweat. Her heart was pounding. It's just a nightmare, she told herself, that's all. She was reassured by the sound of even breathing coming from the sleeping girls around her in the dark bedroom.

But then she realized that the noises from her dream were still going on. The banging sounds had become more like tapping, and there was a soft, but steady roar. They were coming from one direction.

She crawled out of her sleeping bag, climbed over Megan, and tiptoed to the window. Even though it was still dark out, she could see what was causing the noise. Hailstones were popping against the glass pane, and the wind was blowing fiercely.

It's a blizzard, Katie thought. And what had she planned for today? Cross-country skiing. It figured. Now even the weather was conspiring to ruin her week.

But it was silly to blame the weather. Even if it was gorgeous out, they probably couldn't have gone skiing. Sarah's wrenched wrist would have kept her from being able to grip the poles.

And even if her wrist was okay, and they *could* go, Peter and Michael would have wanted to come too. And her friends would have let them.

For a moment, she allowed a wave of self-pity to engulf her. Then she went back to her sleeping bag and climbed in.

But she couldn't sleep. Her body was tired, but her mind was wide-awake. She tried counting sheep. But the sheep refused to be counted—they were running all over the place. She gave up. And she got up and tiptoed out of the room.

The house was silent. Katie padded down the stairs, into the hall, and opened a door. She hit the switch on the wall, and went down another flight to the rec room. Then she made her way to the tiny room off the rec room that her parents used as an office. She sat in the big chair facing the desk and leaned back to think.

The reunion was almost over, and somehow, she had to get things back on track. Her thoughts went back to the night before. After the other girls had gone to sleep, she and Trina had sat on the bed and talked in whispers. Trina had confided in Katie, pouring her heart out about her problems back home with her parents. Katie had listened, and comforted her, and offered a few words of advice that Trina really seemed to appreciate. It had been just like old times back at Sunnyside.

Remembering this gave her hope. She could still make this reunion end with a spectacular finish. Today would be her last chance. If the weather continued the way it was, they'd be trapped indoors all day. She had to come up with a plan.

She took a pad and pen from the desk, and tapped the pen on the pad. What could they do indoors all day? There was that giant puzzle. And the new Wacko game. But she'd mentioned both several times, and never received a very enthusiastic response. If she didn't come up with a creative idea, they'd all be sitting around in front of the television watching soap operas and game shows. Or worse, playing Nintendo with Peter and Michael.

She tried to remember the rainy days at Sunnyside. It seemed like she was always able to come up with some neat indoor activity they could do. The girls would be counting on her to do the same today. She had to show them she hadn't lost the knack. She was still the leader of cabin six. And she would prove it.

It wasn't going to be easy. She racked her brain, trying to come up with something different, unique, really special. C'mon, brain, she pleaded silently. Don't fail me now!

And it didn't. Like the sun beginning to rise outside, an idea dawned on her. And not just any idea. A fantastic one! With firm strokes, on the top of the pad, she scrawled the words "scavenger hunt."

A tingle shot through her. Once, at a town fair, she'd been on a scavenger hunt. It was great fun. That one had involved running all over town. She'd have to come up with items the girls could find right here at home.

Mentally, she explored the house, going from room to room. They needed lots of stuff to search for, so the hunt would take up most of the day, until it was time for their New Year's Eve party. She started down here.

Peering through the door into the rec room, her eyes lit on the Ping-Pong table. She wrote down "Ping-Pong ball." And then, to make it a little harder, she added "cracked."

What else was down here? She snapped her fingers. Her parents' old record collection. She wrote down "Beatles album." And there was the storage room down here. From that she came up with "light bulb" and "battery."

Now for the kitchen. That was easy, and her pen flew across the paper. A tea bag, a dust cloth, a potato with exactly three dark spots. She chuckled as she pictured potatoes all over the floor, the girls frantically picking through them and counting spots.

Her chuckle turned into a sly grin as she considered the twins' bedroom. She could just imagine the boys' horror as five girls poked under their beds and inside drawers, ransacking the room her mother referred to as the disaster area.

Now, what should she make them look for there? She jotted the ideas as they came to her. A red sock. A comic book. A five dollar bill. She strongly suspected that the boys still had money stashed away from their summer lawn mowing.

And then there was her own room. Quickly, she scrawled "a photo from Camp Sunnyside." After the hunt, they could go through them and reminisce. Other items she listed were a headband, an old report card, a shoe lace.

She thought about her parents' bedroom. No, she'd better declare that off-limits.

When she finally had twenty-five items, she stopped. Then she switched on the home computer and started typing the list, carefully pecking out the words and mixing up the items, so the girls would have to run from room to room. Then she printed out five copies.

She glanced at the window. The light coming in told her the sun must be up, though she could barely see it through the snow and the hail. The girls would be waking soon. She couldn't wait to see their faces when they heard what she had planned for them. "Katie, you're brilliant!" they'd cry.

A yawn escaped her lips. She gathered the pages and went back up to her room.

The girls were all in the same positions she'd left them in. Katie slipped the papers under her sleeping bag and climbed back in. Of course, she wouldn't be able to sleep. She was much too excited. But maybe she'd close her eyes for a minute, just to rest them . . .

She opened her eyes, thinking she couldn't wait any longer. She was going to wake them. She sat up, and blinked. She was alone in the room. The beds and the other bags were empty.

Squinting at the clock on the nightstand, she read the time. Ten-thirty! How long had she been sleeping? She jumped up, and she was about to run out of the room when she had an idea, just a little something to help everyone get in the mood.

From her bottom drawer, where she kept her out-of-season clothes, she pulled out a Sunnyside tee shirt and a pair of white shorts. It might be freezing outside, but they'd be in all day and the house was warm.

A glance out the window told her that the hail had stopped, but it was still snowing. She dressed quickly, shoved her feet into sneakers, and went downstairs.

The living room was deserted. Where was everyone? Katie wondered. From the kitchen she heard the sound of running water. Still feeling a little dazed from having slept so late, she gazed blankly at her father who was rinsing off plates in the sink.

"What are you doing home, Dad?"

"The office is closed because of the weather," he told her. He looked at her outfit in amusement. "Looks like I'll be spending the day here at Camp Sunnyside too."

Katie smiled thinly. Home certainly didn't *feel* like Camp Sunnyside at the moment. It was so quiet. "Where is everyone?" she asked.

"Some of the happy campers are outside with your mother. And the others are downstairs playing Ping-Pong."

"Oh." Katie digested this information. She'd have to round them all up. She started toward the door leading down to the rec room, but paused on the way. "Why didn't anyone wake me up for breakfast?"

Her father looked slightly abashed. "To tell the truth, honey, with all your friends around and all the noise, we didn't realize you weren't there with us. We'd just about finished eating when someone asked, where's Katie?"

Unbelievable, Katie thought. How could they not even have noticed that she wasn't there? She, Katie Dillon, who was always the center of everything at Camp Sunnyside?

"And your mother said you must be exhausted, and we should let you sleep," he continued. "Are you hungry? Do you want me to fix you something?"

"No thanks. I need to get things organized for today." She opened the door and heard the sound of a Ping-Pong ball hitting paddles. She hoped whoever was playing would manage to crack a few for the scavenger hunt. She padded halfway down the stairs and leaned over the rail.

Peter and Trina were slamming a ball back and forth, while Megan watched. A ball flew by Peter.

"Sixteen, fifteen, Trina," Megan announced. Trina picked up the ball and went into a serve.

"Hey, you guys, come upstairs," Katie said.

Peter's head turned at the sound of her voice, and he missed a shot.

"Seventeen, fifteen, Trina," Megan said.

"That shouldn't count," Peter objected. "I was distracted."

"Too bad," Megan retorted, grinning.

Katie rapped on the rail. "Megan, Trina," she said insistently. "Come *on*. I've got something planned."

"But I'm winning!" Trina protested. "I have to finish this game."

"And then I get to play the winner," Megan added.

Katie glared at them in frustration. Don't lose your temper, she warned herself. Be nice. But it was getting difficult. "You can have a few more minutes while I get the others," she finally said, but she wasn't even sure they heard her.

Back upstairs, she went through the kitchen to the door that opened to the back yard. Through the window, she could see the bundled figures throwing snowballs at the far end of the yard. She started opening the door.

"Hey, where do you think you're going?" her father asked.

"Outside, to get the others."

"Not like that," he said firmly.

Katie had forgotten she was in her camp clothes. "I'll get a coat."

"Do more than that," Mr. Dillon instructed her. "Put on some long pants and boots if you're going out in that snow. And gloves."

Katie gritted her teeth. But this was one argument she knew she couldn't win. She went back to her room, stripped off her clothes, and pulled on jeans and a sweatshirt. From the hall closet she got her coat, hat, and mittens. And then she headed outside.

Trudging through the freshly falling snow, she

identified the snowball fighters—her mother, Michael, Erin, and Sarah. Seeing was believing, but Katie was still floored. Erin, who wouldn't walk out the door of cabin six without makeup on and her hair looking perfect—there she was with snow matting down her hair and her jacket displaying evidence of having been struck with a number of balls.

And Sarah, who had to be dragged and coaxed into doing anything physical, was packing snow with her one good hand while being bombarded by Michael with balls.

Her mother was the only one who seemed to see Katie standing there. "Hi, sweetie! Which team do you want to be on?"

Katie shook her head. "I want everyone to come inside. I've got something planned for us."

At that moment, one of Erin's snowballs hit Michael right in the face, leaving him momentarily stunned. Everyone started laughing at his expression.

"Come inside," Katie repeated.

"In a second," Sarah called.

Katie stood there uncertainly. "Well, okay."

Back in the house, she removed her coat. Then she went up to her room and changed back into her Sunnyside outfit. She got the scavenger hunt sheets out from under the sleeping bag and went over them. She wanted to be completely prepared when she presented her idea.

At least she didn't have to drag them all into the living room. When she got back downstairs, they were there. But they weren't waiting for her.

Peter and her father were pulling out the legs of a card table. Another table was already set up. Erin and Megan were arranging chairs around them. Her mother and Trina were setting up a Monopoly game, and Sarah was counting out the play money. Michael emerged from the rec room with a Scrabble game in his hands.

"What's going on?" Katie asked.

"We're having a games competition," Megan told her. "Monopoly and Scrabble."

"Whose idea was that?"

"Mine," Trina said, smiling. "It'll be like the activities hall on a rainy day at Sunnyside."

"But I've got something else for us to do," Katie told them. "It's a scavenger hunt."

"We can do that after the games," Sarah said.

After the games? Katie frowned. Monopoly and Scrabble took forever!

Mr. Dillon was rubbing his hands gleefully as he looked down at the Monopoly board. "As someone who actually works in real estate, I think I've got an edge on you guys."

"Don't count on that," Erin said, laughing. "I'm into money!"

Katie felt sick. And she felt even worse as she counted the chairs around the two tables. Eight. Her mother, father, Peter, Michael, Megan, Erin, Sarah, Trina—that made eight. What about her? Had they completely forgotten she was there?

At least her very own mother acknowledged her existence. "Get another chair, Katie."

Katie stood stiffly. "No, thanks. I don't want to play." But they were all chattering and laughing, and no one heard her.

She turned and went back upstairs to her room. Sitting on her bed, she pulled up her knees and wrapped her arms around them. In two minutes, her mother, or somebody, would realize she wasn't there. Whoever it was would come upstairs and want to know what was wrong. And how was she going to reply?

Everything was wrong. They were making plans without her. Nobody was listening to her or paying attention to her. She could even not be there, and nobody would notice the difference.

They didn't need her anymore. They didn't even want her. A combination of hurt and anger and sadness churned inside her.

"Oh, I wish I didn't know any of them," she

103

said aloud with passion. "I wish I'd never even gone to Sunnyside at all." She buried her face in her hands and sobbed.

She cried until there were no tears left, but she remained in that position, her hands over her face. And then, in the silence of the room, there came a soft voice.

"Your wish is granted."

She hadn't heard anyone come in. Unwilling to move, Katie asked, "Who's that? What did you say?"

The voice came again. It was strange, unfamiliar. "Your wish is granted."

Katie raised her head slightly and spread her fingers to peek through them. No one was there.

It wasn't her imagination. She *had* heard something. A cold chill penetrated her body. "Who said that?"

"I did."

Slowly, Katie turned her head in the direction of the voice. Her eyes rested on the big doll in Sunnyside clothes, sitting on the top of her bookcase. No, she told herself. It's impossible. Her mind was playing tricks on her.

But she couldn't take her eyes off the doll. And then the doll blinked.

Katie swallowed. "What—what did you say?"

There was no denying what happened next. The doll's lips moved. "I'm going to grant your wish." Then she slid off the bookcase and floated to the floor.

Strangely enough, Katie wasn't frightened. This is a dream, she thought. I've fallen asleep and I'm having a dream.

"What do you want?" Katie asked, surprised to hear her own voice calm and steady, not even trembling.

The doll approached her. When she spoke again, her voice was testy. "Aren't you listening? I *said*, I'm going to grant your wish."

"What wish?"

The doll gave her a look which strongly suggested Katie was an idiot. "The wish you just made! You said, and I quote, 'I wish I didn't know any of them. I wish I'd never even gone to Sunnyside at all.' Well, I can make that wish come true." She waved a hand in the air. "Poof! You don't know any of them. And you've never been to Camp Sunnyside."

Katie shifted uneasily on her bed. This was the weirdest dream she'd ever had. She wasn't sure she liked it. Abruptly, she got off her bed.

"Where are you going?" the doll demanded.

"Downstairs. To play games with my friends."

"They're not there," the doll informed her.

"What do you mean, they're not there?"

"Just what I said. Your friends from cabin six

105

are not downstairs. If you don't believe me, go see for yourself."

That was exactly what Katie intended to do. She swept past the doll and walked out the door. This is ridiculous, she thought as she made her way down the stairs. But when she reached the bottom, she caught her breath.

There were no card tables in the living room, and no games going on. Her father was lying on the sofa, taking a nap. Her mother was sitting in a chair with the newspaper. Peter and Michael were planted in front of the television, playing Nintendo. There was no sign of Megan, Sarah, Trina, or Erin.

She ran back upstairs. And when she returned to her bedroom, she noticed something else. The sleeping bags were gone. So were the suitcases.

The doll was still standing there. Now her arms were folded across her chest and she was tapping one foot impatiently. "Now do you believe me?"

Katie's head was spinning. "This is crazy! Where did everyone go?"

"They were never here," the doll replied. "Boy, are you dense. Think about it. If you never went to camp, and you never knew any of them, you wouldn't be inviting them to a reunion, would you?"

Katie sank down on her bed. "I don't get it. Who are you, anyway?"

The doll shrugged. "I guess you can call me your fairy godmother. Or something like that. It doesn't matter. What's important is that you got your wish."

Katie fixed a hard, cold stare on the doll. "I don't believe you."

The doll sighed. "I was afraid of that. You're so bullheaded. I had a feeling you were going to need more convincing. Come on." She held out her hand.

"Where are we going?" Katie asked.

"To Camp Sunnyside."

Katie gasped. "In the middle of winter?"

"Look, I'm a fairy godmother, right? Or whatever. Anyway, I've got magic."

"That's silly," Katie stated. "There's no such thing as magic."

The doll responded with a smug smile. "Wanna bet? Take my hand."

Katie eyed the outstretched arm uneasily. Oh, what the heck? she thought. It's just a dream. I might as well see it through. She placed her own hand in the doll's.

And then, everything around her went fuzzy— her bookcase, the desk, all the objects in her room seemed to dissolve. The walls of the room faded. She wasn't even sitting on her bed anymore. She was floating in space, her legs dangling, nothing beneath her. Her grip on the doll's hand tightened.

This was getting weirder and weirder. She was traveling, but she wasn't moving. She saw nothing, yet she wasn't in darkness. She shut her eyes. I'll wake up in a minute, she told herself.

Then she felt her feet planted firmly on the ground. And the doll spoke.

"You can open your eyes now. We're here."

Chapter 7

Opening her eyes wasn't enough. Katie had to pinch herself to believe what she saw. And even with that, she stood there in stunned disbelief. But there was no doubt about it. She was at Camp Sunnyside.

She and the doll were on the landing by the swimming pool. Girls in bathing suits brushed by her. In the water, campers were yelling and swimming and racing each other.

As she absorbed the sights and sounds, Katie thought, if this is a dream, it's awfully real. When one girl jumped off the ledge near her into the pool, Katie felt the spray of water from the splash she made.

A surge of excitement filled her. "I can't believe it!" she said to the doll. "I'm really here! This is our pool! Usually we have swimming lessons here every morning, but this must be a free swim day." She gazed around the landing.

"Look! There's Darrell!" She put one hand over her heart as she used the other to point out the handsome swimming coach. Her eyes swept over the girls in the water. Then she clutched the doll's hand.

"There's Trina!" she squealed. "Trina's my best friend at Sunnyside." She searched for other familiar faces. "And over there, on the opposite side, that's Megan. She's a nut, really funny. Sometimes she keeps us up half the night laughing. Watch her do this dive. She's very good."

"She doesn't look so good to me," the doll commented as Megan entered the pool with a belly flop.

"She's usually better," Katie said. "Yuck, here comes Maura Kingsley and the cabin nine girls. Maura thinks she's the queen of Sunnyside, but she's truly awful. Watch, she'll say something really nasty to me." But to her surprise, Maura sauntered by without a word.

"I wish I had my bathing suit on," Katie said, eyeing the water hungrily. "Maybe I could run back to the cabin real quick and get it."

"It won't do any good," the doll said. "Your bathing suit's not there."

"Huh?" Katie was distracted by the sound of

Darrell's whistle. "It's too late anyway. Swim period's over." She watched as Trina climbed out of the pool. "Trina! Over here!" She waved her hand in the air.

Trina came around the side and glanced at her curiously. "Yes? What do you want?"

"Nothing special," Katie replied. "Hi, Megan!"

The little redhead blinked. "Hi."

Trina turned to Megan. "I saw you trying to dive. What happened?"

Megan frowned. "It was that girl standing next to me. She was looking at me funny. I think she put a curse on me to ruin my dive."

Katie started laughing. "Oh, Megan, you're so funny sometimes!"

Megan was still frowning as she turned back to Katie. "How do you know my name?"

Katie poked the doll. "See? She's a riot!"

Trina and Megan looked at each other, and shrugged. Then the two of them started walking away.

"Hey," Katie called, hurrying after them. "Wait up! You want to go get ice cream?"

"That's where we're going," Trina said. "You can come if you want." Then, politely, she asked, "Are you new around here?"

Katie had forgotten the doll was still by her side. "Oh, this is . . . this is . . ."

"You can call me Dolly," the doll said.

"And what's your name?" Trina asked Katie.

Katie started laughing again. Trina eyed her quizzically, and then spoke to Megan. "Was that funny?"

They had reached the ice cream stand. Trina ordered a chocolate chip cone. "I'll have vanilla," Katie said. "You want strawberry, right, Megan?"

"Well, yeah, but . . ."

Katie explained to the doll. "Megan loves strawberry."

"How'd you know that?" Megan asked.

"Because you *always* get strawberry! Hey, where are the others?"

"What others?" Trina asked.

Katie was nonplussed. "Well, Erin and—"

Trina's eyes went cold. "Are you a friend of Erin's?"

"Of course! We all are!"

Megan stepped back. "If you're a friend of Erin's, we don't want you hanging around with us. C'mon, Trina."

Katie gaped at their departing figures. "What's the matter with them?"

"They don't know you," the doll said.

"That's ridiculous," Katie replied. "Of

course they know me. We've known each other for years!" Then she grinned. "Wait, I get it. This is some sort of game they're playing. Yeah, that's it. It's a joke they're pulling on me."

"You really think so?" the doll asked.

"Sure! They never act that weird."

"If you think that was weird," the doll commented, "you haven't seen anything yet."

That's a strange thing to say, Katie thought. But what could she expect from a doll? "I'm going back to the cabin," she announced. The doll walked beside her. Along the way, Katie pointed out various sights. "That's the activities hall. The dining hall is just beyond it. Down that slope are the tennis courts."

"You certainly know your way around," the doll remarked.

"Well, I should!" Katie chuckled. "I've been coming here for three summers!"

The doll just smiled.

Katie's step quickened as she approached cabin six. "This is my cabin," she told the doll. "We've all been in the same cabin ever since we started coming here when we were eight." She pushed the door open and went in.

At first, she thought no one was there. She just stood there for a minute, enjoying the

113

warm, comfortable feeling that came from being back in one of her favorite places.

Then she realized someone *was* in the room. She was on a top bunk, Sarah's bed, with a book covering her face. Katie didn't know how she could have missed seeing her when she first walked in. She was really fat. What was she doing on Sarah's bed? Katie wondered.

When the girl raised her head and peered over the book, Katie's mouth fell open.

"Sarah?"

"Yeah?"

"I—I didn't recognize you."

Sarah adjusted her glasses. "I don't recognize you either." She reached a hand into a bag lying by her side, and pulled out a doughnut which she proceeded to devour.

"How come you weren't at the pool?" Katie asked.

"I never go to the pool," Sarah replied.

"Why not?"

"Because I don't like to swim. I'd rather stay here and read. *Alone,*" she added pointedly, and returned to her book.

"This is very strange," Katie said to the doll in an undertone. "How did she get so fat all of a sudden?"

"Because she doesn't get any exercise," the

114

doll explained. "She lies there all day, every day, eating and reading."

"That's not true," Katie protested. "She's been learning how to swim. And she's getting better and better."

"No, she hasn't," the doll said. "And do you know why? Because you haven't been here to encourage her."

The door to the cabin opened and Erin came in. She glanced briefly at Katie and the doll, and then went to the mirror where she began brushing her hair.

"What are you so dressed up for?" Katie asked, taking in Erin's short, tight skirt and halter top.

"If it's any of your business, which it isn't," Erin replied, "I've got a date."

"A date? In the middle of the morning?" Katie looked at the schedule posted by the door. "You can't go on a date. We've got archery now."

Erin raised her eyebrows. "What do you mean, 'we'? Since when are you in this cabin?"

"I've only been here for three summers," Katie sputtered. She looked up at Sarah, expecting her to confirm that, but Sarah was still buried in her book and eating another doughnut. "What kind of date can you have in the morning, anyway?"

Erin picked up her makeup bag and pulled out a lipstick. "Like I said, it's none of your business. But since you're dying of curiosity, I'll tell you. I'm going with some girls from cabin nine to Pine Ridge, and we're meeting some boys from Camp Eagle there."

Katie looked at the schedule again. There was no trip to Pine Ridge listed. "How are you getting there?"

"Hey, what is this, a trial or something? We're hitchhiking, okay?"

"No, it's not okay!" Katie exclaimed. "Erin, that's dangerous!"

Erin looked at her through narrowed eyes. "How did you know my name?"

This game's getting silly, Katie thought. "Because I know you. And if Carolyn finds out—"

"Carolyn? Carolyn who? Oh, you mean that counselor who used to be here."

Puzzled, Katie repeated her words. "Used to be?"

At that very moment, the door to the counselor's room opened. A young woman Katie had never seen before stepped out. "Hasn't that stupid handyman gotten here yet? I still can't get my window open and I'm suffocating."

Neither Erin nor Sarah bothered to answer her. Katie gaped at the woman. "Who are you?"

"I'm the cabin six counselor." Her forehead puckered as she studied Katie and the doll. "Who are you? And what are you doing here?"

Katie fumbled for words. "I—I'm supposed to be here. I mean, this is my cabin."

The counselor groaned. "Oh, no. You mean they're sticking me with two new campers?" She looked out the window. "Thank goodness, here he comes."

Katie stared at the strange woman. What was she doing in cabin six? How could she be the counselor? What happened to Carolyn?

The door opened, and in walked Teddy, the camp handyman. He was one of Katie's favorite people at Sunnyside. He used to be Carolyn's boyfriend, but they'd broken up. They were still good friends, though.

"Hi, Teddy," she said.

"Hi," he responded, smiling the way he smiled at all the campers. But he didn't pause to ruffle Katie's hair the way he usually did.

"Teddy, where's Carolyn?" Katie asked.

His smile faded. "Carolyn?"

"Carolyn! The counselor!"

Now his face became grim. "You mean, the former counselor. Why don't you ask the girls here in cabin six what happened to her?" With that, he went into the counselor's room with the woman. A second later, Katie heard hammering.

"Why did he look at me like that?" Katie asked the doll. "Did I say something wrong?"

"You certainly did," the doll said. "It was very tactless, considering what happened to Carolyn."

Katie looked at her in bewilderment. "I don't understand. What happened to Carolyn?"

"Haven't you figured anything out by now?" the doll asked. She shook her head in disapproval. "It's certainly taking you a long time to catch on."

Katie rubbed her forehead. What was she talking about? This was crazy. Then Erin sauntered past her, heading toward the door. Katie immediately blocked it.

"Erin, don't do it! You could get into major trouble! You know what those cabin nine girls are like!"

Erin glared at her. "Look, I'll say it one more time. Mind your own business! I don't know who you are, but don't you dare tell me what to do. Now, get out of my way!" With a rough hand, she pushed Katie aside and marched out the door.

Katie ran outside after her, and the doll followed. "Erin!" she yelled. But Erin didn't even turn around.

Then she saw Trina and Megan coming up to the cabin. Katie ran to meet them. "Listen, we've got to stop Erin! She's going to hitchhike into Pine Ridge!"

Neither of them looked at all surprised or shocked. Megan shrugged. "So what?"

"So what?! She'll get into trouble!"

"She's always getting into trouble," Megan said. "If you're such a good friend of hers, you should know that."

"We better not stand here talking to this girl," Trina said to Megan. "If she hangs out with Erin, she's just another troublemaker too."

She spoke so seriously that Katie was unnerved. "Trina! You know me better than that!"

Trina's face was a total blank. "I don't know you at all." She tried to walk past her, but Katie blocked her way. "Wait a minute! Maybe if we all go talk to Erin together—"

"We never talk to Erin," Megan stated. "She'd just get us into trouble too. Any day now, she'll be caught again, and this time they'll send her home."

"And I hope that happens soon," Trina commented.

Katie couldn't believe her ears. How could soft-hearted Trina talk like that? And what did

Megan mean when she said they never talked to Erin? Sure, Erin got on everyone's nerves sometimes, but cabin six girls always stuck together.

Trina and Megan moved toward the door, but Katie stopped them. "Wait! Please!"

Now Trina was actually looking annoyed. "What do you want now?"

"Where's Carolyn?"

"Who?"

"Carolyn! Our counselor! Why isn't she here? What happened to her?"

"Oh, *her.*" The way Trina said "her" made it very clear what she thought of Carolyn. "She was fired."

Katie gasped. *"Fired?* Why?"

Trina explained. "She was sneaking out of the cabin late at night, to meet the assistant handyman, Vince. Ms. Winkle found out about it and fired them both."

"But that's not true!" Katie cried out.

"Yes, it is," Trina insisted. "Vince even confessed."

Katie shook her head. "He only did that because he wanted everyone to *think* Carolyn liked him. But the whole story was just a rumor!" She turned to Megan. "You know that. You were the one who started the rumor!"

Megan's face turned a sickly, pale color. "Why—why would I do a thing like that?"

"Because you thought Carolyn was still in love with Teddy. And you figured if Teddy got jealous, that would bring them back together. So you made up a story. You started telling people Carolyn was sneaking out with Vince, so it would get back to Teddy. Don't you remember?"

Trina's eyes widened. She turned to Megan. "Is that true? Did you do that? Jeez, you're even a bigger idiot than I always thought you were."

Megan bit her lip. Then she whirled around and fled into the cabin. Trina ran after her.

"I don't understand!" Katie said to the doll. "Carolyn wasn't fired. Ms. Winkle was going to fire her, but Megan told her she made the whole story up!"

"No, she didn't," the doll said.

"Yes, she did," Katie persisted. "I know! I saw her! I was there!"

"No, you weren't."

Suddenly, Katie's legs felt very weak. She edged over to the steps in front of the cabin and sat down. When she spoke, her voice was shaking. "What . . . what's going on?"

"Megan never confessed to Ms. Winkle," the doll said. "Because you weren't here to persuade her."

"I didn't have to persuade her," Katie argued. "She *wanted* to confess."

"She needed your support."

"But it wasn't just me," Katie said. "The other girls agreed she should go tell Ms. Winkle."

"No, they didn't," the doll said. "You see, they don't talk to each other very much. They're all so different. They just fight all the time. And there's no one here to help bring them together."

"What about Trina? She doesn't fight. She tries to help everyone get along."

"No, she doesn't," the doll disagreed. "You see, Trina's had a lot of problems at home, with her parents' divorce. She's had no one to talk with about these problems. And when you don't have a best friend to talk with, the problems build up inside you. You get angry and sullen and bitter. That's what's happened to Trina. She's not a happy person."

"Yes, she is," Katie argued stubbornly. "This is some weird trick you're playing on me. That wasn't really Trina. And that wasn't Megan! That's not the way they act. I *know* them!"

"No, you don't." The doll's voice became gentle. "You got your wish, Katie. You've never

122

been to Sunnyside. You don't know any of these girls. And none of them knows you."

Katie leaped up and glared at her in fury. "I don't believe you!"

The doll gave an exasperated sigh. "I was afraid it wouldn't be this easy. Come on." She held out her hand. "I can see you're going to need more convincing."

❄ Chapter 8

Katie didn't want to go anywhere with this crazy doll. But somehow, her hand found its way into the doll's hand. And once again, everything around her went fuzzy and began to dissolve. She couldn't look, so she shut her eyes. Like the first time, she felt herself floating.

When her feet were once again planted on firm ground, Katie asked, "Can I open my eyes now?"

"Shh," the doll hissed. And in a whisper, she said, "Yes, you can look."

When Katie opened her eyes, she saw why the doll had hushed her. They were in the dining hall, but the large room wasn't in its usual noisy, chaotic condition. The tables were gone, and the chairs were set up in rows. All the seats were occupied, and all eyes were on the stage.

A group of very young campers were up there, performing a folk dance. They looked cute, Katie thought. But what was she doing here? Why did she need to see this? She noticed that the audience wasn't made up entirely of Sunnyside people. There were kids wearing tee shirts from several other camps in the area. Then it hit her.

"It's the Sunnyside Spectacular," she murmured in wonderment. She explained in a whisper to the doll. "It's like a variety show. Groups put on different acts. We invite other camps to come watch it. We're putting on a play that Sarah wrote." She scrutinized the act on stage. "In fact, we're on next. I should be backstage."

"Why?" the doll asked.

"Because I'm the director."

The doll shook her head wearily. "You didn't direct the play, Katie. You weren't *here* to direct it."

The young campers finished their dance to a burst of applause. Then Ms. Winkle stepped out onto the stage and spoke to the audience.

"Our next presentation is an original play written by Sarah Fine, and performed by campers from cabin five and cabin six. It's called 'The Search for Happiness.' "

"No, it isn't," Katie said softly. "We changed the name of the play to 'The Battle of the Spirits,' so it would sound more exciting."

"Whose idea was that?" the doll asked.

"Mine."

The doll smiled in an obnoxiously smug way. "Then it was never changed."

The curtain rose on four girls playing London

Bridge Is Falling Down. On one side of the stage stood Erin, pointing a wand at the four girls.

Katie couldn't help smiling as she heard the familiar opening lines. She remembered them so well, she moved her lips along with the speakers.

"Isn't this fun?" one girl said.

Another replied, "Yes, we always have fun together."

The third girl spoke. "It's nice that we always have good times together and never fight."

Wait a minute, Katie thought. Something was wrong. "Megan's supposed to be up there," she said.

"Who cast the show?" the doll asked.

Katie sighed. "I did."

The fourth girl was saying, "That's because we have the Spirit of Happiness with us."

Erin, as the Spirit of Happiness, stepped forward. Actually, she swaggered, swaying her hips. In a deep, sexy voice, she drawled, "And I will always be with you to keep you happy and joyful and friends forever."

The audience tittered. Katie grimaced. "That's not how she's supposed to say it."

At the sound of the tittering, Erin stepped out of character and made a face at the audience. The giggles turned into actual laughter.

It got worse. Katie moaned when she saw Megan come out onto the stage as the Spirit of Meanness. "Oh, no. Why would anyone let Megan play that part? She can't remember lines!"

Megan proved her point. "Uh, I'm the Spirit of Meanness." The goofy grin on her face made her look anything but mean. "And, um, wait a minute . . . oh yeah. There won't be any more, you know, happiness in this land. For I, the Spirit of Meanness . . ." She paused to giggle. "Right, I'm the Spirit of Meanness and I'm in charge now. And my power is . . . is . . . well, I got a lot of it."

"This is awful!" Katie declared, louder than she'd intended. But it didn't matter. The laughter from the audience was so loud now, no one could hear her.

Katie watched in horror as the play staggered along. It was a disaster. At the very end, the girls crowded around Erin for her final speech. Again, Erin spoke in that phony voice.

"Remember, if you love each other, if you care about each other—hey, quit pushing me! What was I saying? Oh, yeah, blah, blah, blah, if you care about each other, you'll never lose me. Ow! You stepped on my toe!"

By now, the audience was roaring. The only sound that could be hear above the laughter was the occasional boo.

Katie covered her face. "This is humiliating!

128

I can't bear it! How will I be able to face anyone?"

"You won't need to," the doll told her. "You had nothing to do with this play. And what do you care anyway? These aren't your friends. Want to see more?"

She didn't wait for a response before grabbing Katie's hand. The room blurred, Katie shut her eyes, and then came the floating sensation. When she could see again, she found herself on the banks of the lake, with the doll, behind a rock.

It was night, a crystal clear night in which each star was a pinpoint of light. Katie shivered a little from the cool night air, and stepped closer to the huge bonfire burning brightly on the lakefront.

Now, what was this? she wondered. As soon as her eyes adjusted to the darkness, she figured it out. On one side of the bonfire, the campers wore blue headbands. On the other side, they were wearing red ones.

Katie clapped her hands. "It's color war!" Hurriedly, she explained to the doll. "The camp is divided into two teams, the blues and the reds. We have all sorts of competitions. I better get over there. I'm captain of the blues."

Before the doll could say her usual "no, you're not," Katie ran away from her and sat down with the blue team. Nobody noticed her, because their eyes were on Ms. Winkle, standing in the center of the crowd.

"Of course, there are no losers at Sunnyside," Ms. Winkle was saying to them. "But as in all competitions, there is one team which excels, and I will now announce the name of that team. The winner of this summer's Sunnyside color war is . . ." She paused dramatically, holding on to the suspense as long as possible. "The red team!"

Katie's mouth dropped open. That was impossible! She gaped as that horrible Maura Kingsley rose and strode up to Ms. Winkle to accept the trophy for her team. Katie leaped up and ran back to the doll.

"This is all wrong! *They* didn't win color war! The blue team won!"

The doll shook her head. "They didn't win, Katie. You weren't here to lead them."

Katie looked back at the blue team. Their heads were bowed, and they all looked really down. It was very upsetting. "I want to get out of here," she told the doll.

The doll promptly took her hand. "Let's go."

By now, Katie was used to what was about to happen. The scene began to blur, and she shut her eyes, waiting to float. Only she didn't, this time.

When she opened her eyes, the bonfire was gone, and so were the campers, but she and the doll were still in the same place behind the rock on the lakefront.

"I told you I wanted to get out of here," Katie said. "Why are we staying?"

"Something's about to happen that I thought you should see," the doll said.

There was nothing to see as far as Katie could tell. There was the deserted lakefront, with the empty canoes resting on the bank. It was a pretty sight, Katie thought with longing. The reflection of the crescent moon on the water glimmered, and it was all so peaceful, so quiet . . .

Then the peace was broken by the sound of hushed giggles and whispers. Katie squinted in the direction of the noise. A bunch of girls, five of them, were coming down the slope.

As they got closer, Katie recognized them. They were the girls from cabin nine, Maura's crowd, all thirteen-year-old girls who thought they were terribly cool. Katie crouched behind the rock so they wouldn't see her.

The doll was watching her closely, and she must have seen something in Katie's expression. "You don't like those girls, do you?"

"No," Katie said vehemently. "They think they're better than everyone else, but they're

131

really jerks. Erin thought they were cool, but that's just because they wear makeup and talk about boys all the time. She was always trying to hang out with them."

"Did they let her?" the doll asked.

"Yeah, but they were just using her," Katie told the doll. "They tried to get her to do stupid things. Like, they wanted to get rid of one of their cabin mates, Phyllis. They told Erin to sneak into Ms. Winkle's office and put demerits on Phyllis's record in the computer."

"Did Erin do it?"

"No. I caught her, just when she was about to sneak into Ms. Winkle's window, and I talked her out of doing it." She paused. "Erin really didn't want to do it. She's not that awful. She just needed to hear someone else say it was wrong."

"Someone like you?"

Katie nodded. "Yeah. I guess so." She watched as the cabin nine girls began dragging a canoe toward the water.

"What are they doing?" the doll asked.

Katie scowled. "Probably sneaking over to Camp Eagle. They're so dumb. They could all get sent home for that. Actually, they deserve it, the way they treat poor Phyllis."

"You don't have to worry about Phyllis anymore," the doll said.

"What do you mean?"

"She's not here at Camp Sunnyside now. She was sent home for having too many demerits on her record."

Katie was stunned. "But—I just told you—"

The doll's eyes bore into her own. "You weren't there to talk Erin out of doing it."

Katie felt sick. Then the doll said, "Look."

Erin was coming down the slope. She waved to the cabin nine girls. They waved back. Katie caught her breath.

"She's not going to go with them, is she?"

"Why wouldn't she?"

"No!" Katie couldn't stand it any longer. She ran out from behind the rock. "Erin!"

Erin stopped. When she saw who was speaking, she scowled. "Oh. It's *you*. What do you want now?"

"You're not going to cross the lake with those girls, are you?"

"What's it to you?" Erin asked sharply.

"Erin, it's wrong! It's against the rules!"

Erin tossed her head nonchalantly. "We don't care about rules."

"But Erin, you could get sent home if you're caught," Katie pleaded. "We don't want to lose you!"

"What do you mean, 'we'?"

"We! Us! Cabin six!"

133

Erin put her hands on her hips. "First of all, you're not even *in* cabin six. And secondly, I don't care about the rest of the cabin six girls. They don't even talk to me anyway. Besides, now that Phyllis is gone, I'm moving into cabin nine."

"Erin!" the girls by the canoe called.

"I'm coming!" To Katie, she said, "You're starting to bug me. Get lost!"

Then Katie saw something behind Erin, on the slope. Not something. Some one. It was Teddy, the handyman, holding a flashlight.

The cabin nine girls must have seen him too. Suddenly, they all took off, running away from the canoe into the shadows.

Erin turned. "Where did everyone go?"

The beam from Teddy's flashlight hit Erin in the face. She covered her eyes. Katie jumped back behind the rock.

"Hold it right there!" Teddy yelled. He scrambled down the slope and grabbed Erin by the arm. "You're in serious trouble, young lady. Come with me."

Katie watched as he pulled Erin up toward the road. "Ohmigosh. I've got to tell the others." As soon as the figures of Teddy and Erin disappeared, she started running up the slope. The doll was close behind.

Katie was out of breath when she reached

cabin six. She pushed the door open and went into the dark room. "Wake up, you guys!"

"What's going on?" Megan asked sleepily.

"It's Erin! She's in trouble!"

Trina pulled herself up on her elbows. "What's new about that?"

"I mean it," Katie stated. "It's serious! She got caught trying to sneak across the lake."

"Who cares?" Sarah mumbled.

"We care!" Katie insisted. "We have to help her!"

"I'm not helping her," Megan said. "I hope she gets sent home. Erin's bad. I think she might even be a witch."

"Oh, Megan," Katie said in disgust. "You don't really believe that. There's no such thing as a witch."

"There is too," Megan said indignantly. "We had one right here at camp for a while. A day camper. She had a black cat, and she always wore this locket that she used to cast spells on people."

"Are you talking about Tanya?" Katie asked.

"Yeah! She could predict every day what we were going to have for lunch. And she made me fall down and hurt my ankle. And she tripped my horse—" Megan stopped suddenly. "Hey, how did you know her name?"

"Because I remember her," Katie said impatiently. "And she wasn't a witch. You know that, Megan."

"How could you remember her?" Trina asked. "You weren't even here!"

Even in the darkness, Katie could see the frightened look on Megan's face.

"Maybe you're a witch too!" she cried out. "Maybe both of you are!"

Katie stamped her foot. "Megan, that's ridiculous! It's me, Katie Dillon!"

"I never heard of anyone named Katie Dillon," Sarah said.

"Neither have I," said Trina. "But you seem to know everything about us." She got out of bed. "Maybe Megan's right. Maybe you *are* a witch!"

"Trina!" Katie cried out in protest.

Trina grabbed Katie by the arm with one hand, and the doll with the other. "Get out of here! Both of you!" And with a strength Katie didn't even know Trina had, she pushed them both out the door. And slammed it shut.

Katie was so shaken she couldn't move. Trina, her best friend, had just thrown her out of the cabin. And what was all that nonsense about witches?

"I don't understand," she said brokenly. "Megan always had a wild imagination, but—"

136

The doll interrupted. "But you guys were always able to keep it under control, right?"

"Yeah! She'd go off on one of her crazy fantasies, like with Tanya, but we could always get her out of it."

"It was you, most of all, Katie," the doll said. "You helped Megan keep one foot on earth. Without you around, there's been nothing to curb her imagination from running wild."

Katie stood there silently, and absorbed this. Poor Megan, frightened by her own imagination. Sarah, fat and lonely. Trina, angry and mean and not even willing to help Erin . . .

"Erin!" Katie turned to the doll. "I have to find out what's happening to her. Come on."

Walking rapidly, she led the doll across the campgrounds to Ms. Winkle's cabin. It was late, but she could see through the windows that lights were on inside. Katie went up to the door and rapped lightly. When there was no response, she pushed the door open.

The reception room was empty, but the door leading to Ms. Winkle's private office was slightly ajar. In there, Katie could see Erin sitting slumped in a chair. And she could hear Ms. Winkle's voice. "This is disgraceful, Erin! I've warned you over and over about breaking the rules. This time you've gone too far!"

Katie chewed on a fingernail. She knew Ms.

Winkle could lecture for hours before she got to the point. She looked around the reception room. Her eyes settled on one of the many framed photographs sitting on Ms. Winkle's desk. It was a picture of a girl about Katie's age with short dark hair. Katie picked it up and studied it.

"Is she a camper here?" the doll asked.

"She was, for a few weeks," Katie replied. "She's Ms. Winkle's niece, Jackie. She stayed in our cabin."

"Did you like her?"

"Not at first," Katie admitted. "She acted real mean, like a gangster or something. She wanted us to think she was tough. She complained about everything at camp. And she was always going on about her life back in New York, how she was in a gang and they shoplifted from stores."

"She doesn't sound like a very nice girl," the doll remarked.

"We didn't think so, either," Katie said. "Especially when things started disappearing at camp. We thought she was the thief. Only Sarah didn't believe that. She kept saying Jackie was putting on an act, because she had problems. She said, deep inside Jackie was really a nice girl. And Sarah turned out to be right."

From the inner office, Ms. Winkle's voice became louder. "You've had your last warning,

Erin. I won't put up with your behavior any longer. I've already called your parents, and they're on their way here to get you." With that, Ms. Winkle came out of the office and shut the door behind her.

"What are you girls doing here at this hour?" she asked Katie and the doll.

"I—we were worried about Erin," Katie said.

Ms. Winkle frowned. "You should be in your cabins. What's your name?"

"Katie Dillon."

Ms. Winkle went behind her desk and flipped through the file. "There's no Katie Dillon registered at this camp."

"But I *do* go to this camp," Katie insisted. "I've been coming here for three summers. Ms. Winkle, you have to remember me!"

Ms. Winkle stared at her. "I've never seen you before."

"Yes, you have!" Katie insisted. "I'm in cabin six! I've *always* been in cabin six! I know Erin, and Trina, and Megan, and Sarah, and . . . and . . ." She held up the photo. "I know your niece, Jackie!"

Ms. Winkle gasped. "You do?"

"Of course!"

Ms. Winkle put a hand to her mouth. "Then— then you must be from the reform school too."

"Reform school! What reform school?"

Ms. Winkle's hand was shaking. "The reform school Jackie was sent to when we found out she'd been stealing from the cabins here."

"But she wasn't stealing!" Katie cried out.

The doll spoke. "Everyone thought she was the thief, Katie. You see, Sarah never befriended her."

"Why not?"

"Because Sarah never became friends with anyone. Because you weren't here to get her off her bed. You see, Katie, it's not just what you did at Sunnyside that never happened. It's also what other people did who were influenced by you."

"What are you talking about?" Ms. Winkle asked in bewilderment. "And where did you get Sunnyside tee shirts? Did you steal them?"

Katie didn't know what to say. It didn't matter. Ms. Winkle put her hand on the phone.

"I think you're a runaway from that reform school," she said. "I'm calling the camp security guards."

"No, Ms. Winkle, don't," Katie pleaded. "I belong here!"

"Send a guard here immediately," Ms. Winkle said into the phone.

Katie turned to the doll in alarm. "What are we going to do?" Before the doll could respond, a man in a uniform entered the office.

"They're runaways from the reform school!" Ms. Winkle announced. "Take them back there!"

The man grabbed Katie and the doll. "No, no," Katie yelled. "I'm not a runaway! This is my camp!" As she struggled with the guard, she tried to sing. " 'I'm a Sunnyside girl with a Sunnyside smile, and I spend my summers in Sunnyside style!' "

"Don't sing that song!" Ms. Winkle ordered her. "You have no business singing that song!"

"But I do, I do!" Katie shrieked. "I'm a Sunnyside girl!" She punched the guard and kicked him. He didn't even seem to feel it. In a panic, she held out her free hand toward the doll. "Do something!"

"What do you want me to do?"

"Make—make everything right again!" With all her might, she extended her hand farther, trying to reach the doll's hand. It wasn't easy, with the guard holding them apart. But somehow, by straining and pushing, their hands met.

And Katie had never before felt such relief as she felt when the room began to blur.

Chapter 9

"I'm a Sunnyside girl," Katie repeated, over and over. "I'm a Sunnyside girl." She clutched the doll's hand tightly. "I'm Katie Dillon from cabin six! I am! I am!"

Even with her eyes closed, images passed before her. The Spectacular, color war, Erin in Ms. Winkle's office, Trina shoving her out of the cabin . . . she could still feel that rough hand gripping her arm. Was it the guard, or was it Trina? Her body was floating, her head was spinning, and she was so confused.

She forced herself to open her eyes and look. It was Trina whose hand was on her arm. She was shoving her, pushing her, shaking her. Well, Katie wasn't going to take it anymore.

"Get your hands off me!" she yelled. She grabbed Trina's wrist and forced it away.

Trina pulled back. "But I was just—"

"I don't care!" Katie exclaimed. She sat up. "Don't you dare try to push me around, Trina

143

Sandburg. And don't you ever speak to me that way again! I don't care how bad your problems are, you can't treat people like that!"

Trina looked like she'd been slapped in the face. "Like—like what?"

"Acting like you don't care about people! Throwing me out of the cabin!"

"Katie, what are you talking about?"

Then Megan was there too. "What's going on in here?"

Katie turned toward her. "And for your information, I am *not* a witch!"

Megan's face was all innocence. "Who said you were?"

Behind her, Erin appeared. "Who's yelling?"

Katie gasped. "Erin, you're still here!"

"Where else would I be?" she asked.

"But you were sent home . . ."

"I was?"

And then Katie saw that she wasn't in cabin six or Ms. Winkle's office or anywhere at Camp Sunnyside. She was in her very own room, at home, sitting on her very own bed.

"Katie? Are you all right?" Trina asked. Her sweet face was marked with lines of concern.

"I'm fine," Katie said automatically. Then her eyes widened. "Hey! You called me Katie!"

Trina smiled uncertainly. "Well, that's your name, isn't it?"

"Yes," Katie affirmed. "I'm Katie Dillon." She turned to the others. "Right?"

"Absolutely," Megan said, and Erin nodded.

"And . . . and you all know me, right?"

"Only for three years!" Erin said. "Katie, what's the matter with you?"

But Katie wasn't finished. "And we all go to Camp Sunnyside every summer, and we stay in cabin six, right?"

Trina, Megan, and Erin exchanged mystified looks. "Right," they chorused.

"And our counselor is named Carolyn. And last summer the blue team won the color war, right?"

"Right," they said again.

Megan plunked herself on the bed. "Katie, did you have a bad dream or something?"

"A bad dream," Katie repeated. She rubbed her forehead. "I don't know. It was so real."

Sarah came in and joined the group. "What's up?"

"Katie had a nightmare," Trina told her.

Was that all it was? Katie wondered. Then she noticed Sarah. "You're not fat anymore."

Sarah eyed her indignantly. "I've *never* been fat. A little chubby, maybe, but not *fat.*"

"Do you want to tell us about your dream?" Megan asked. "Sometimes you feel better if you talk about it."

145

"I . . . I was back at Sunnyside. And you all were there. But you didn't know me. It was like I'd never been there before. I was a stranger."

Erin gawked at her. "A stranger at Sunnyside? *You?*"

Sarah shook her head. "No way. It wouldn't be Sunnyside without you, Katie."

"Why do you say that?" Katie asked.

"Because you're the center of everything at Sunnyside," Sarah said. "You're like our leader!"

Megan nodded fervently. "That's right. You always have the best ideas."

"And you're always taking over," Erin added.

"If it wasn't for you," Trina said, "Sunnyside would be boring."

"Yeah, I would never have learned how to swim," Sarah noted. She grinned. "I'd probably be lying in bed all day reading and eating candy."

"Doughnuts," Katie murmured.

"And I'd be daydreaming all the time," Megan remarked.

"I probably wouldn't even be there," Erin said. "I'll bet I would have gotten into so much trouble, Ms. Winkle would have sent me home ages ago."

"But that's exactly what happened!" Katie

146

exclaimed. "At least, that's what I *thought* happened."

"It must have been an awful dream," Trina said soothingly. "And not just for you, for all of us! Why, if you weren't at Sunnyside, I don't know how I'd feel. I don't think I'd be the same person."

"You weren't," Katie said. Impulsively, she reached out and hugged Trina. And suddenly everyone was on her bed, hugging one another. Even Erin.

"Sunnyside wouldn't be the same for me either, without you guys," Katie said. "It'll be awful next summer if you don't come back."

Sarah hesitated. "I haven't really decided whether or not I want to apply for the honors program. I might be back at Sunnyside."

Trina's head bobbed up and down. "I think I'm going to tell my father we have to take our trip *after* the camp session."

"I suppose there's a chance they'll get a real tennis coach at Sunnyside," Megan said. "Then I wouldn't have to go to a special camp."

"What about you, Erin?" Katie asked.

"I'd still rather go to France or Italy. But I'll think about it."

It was the most they could hope for from Erin.

Katie sighed happily. "How did the games go downstairs?"

Sarah wrinkled her nose. "It got boring after a while."

"Yeah," Megan said. "And I think your brothers were cheating."

Katie could believe that. "They always do."

"You said you had something special planned for us," Trina commented.

"It's a scavenger hunt," Katie told them.

Megan brightened. "That sounds like fun."

"But my brothers can't play," Katie cautioned them. "Because they'd already know where everything is."

"They're not home anyway," Erin said, sighing. "I think they went over to a friend's."

Sarah giggled. "Yeah, Peter got mad because he was having a hard time at Scrabble. Just between us, he doesn't have a very good vocabulary."

"And they were teasing us a lot, too," Megan said.

Trina agreed. "I think they're getting tired of having us around."

"Speak for yourself," Erin declared.

"But how are you going to play?" Megan asked Katie. "You'll know where everything is too."

"I'll direct the hunt," Katie said.

"That's what you're best at," Trina noted.

Katie scrambled off the bed. "Okay, you guys go down to the living room, and I'll be there in a minute." They all started out of the bedroom.

"Hey, Sarah," Katie called.

Sarah looked back over her shoulder. "What?"

"Remember what you told us your father says? Something about, be careful what you wish for because you might get it?"

Sarah nodded.

"Well, he was right."

Sarah gave her a puzzled look before following the others out.

Alone in the room, Katie looked around for her scavenger hunt lists. Where had she left them? As her eyes roamed the room, they settled on her bookcase.

The doll was still there, just where Katie had put her before the girls came. She moved closer and touched the doll's arm.

It was just a doll, nothing more. Gazing at her, Katie knew for certain she couldn't move or speak or listen. But she spoke to her anyway.

"That wasn't the best dream I've ever had. But I suppose I needed to have it. I mean, I learned something. I found out that people need me, even if they don't always act like they do. And I *am* important. But I guess I shouldn't expect to be important every minute of every day."

"Katie, aren't you coming?" Trina stood in the doorway.

"Sure. I just have to find the scavenger hunt lists."

Trina came in. "Who were you talking to just now?"

"Just myself," Katie said. "Oh, there are the lists." She grabbed them from the nightstand. "Okay, let's go."

Trina was looking at the doll. "That's weird."

"What is?" Katie asked.

"Didn't you tell me your grandmother just sent you this for Christmas?"

"Yeah. Why?"

"Her feet are dirty."

"They are?" Katie came closer and examined the bottoms of the doll's feet. Sure enough, there were marks of brown and green on them.

Trina laughed. "They look like my sneakers at camp, all covered with dirt and grass stains. It almost looks like she's been walking around outside."

"Yeah," Katie said. "It must be from the wrapping paper she came in."

"Come on, everyone's waiting," Trina said, and went out the door. Katie followed, but she paused at the door and looked back at the doll thoughtfully. Then she smiled.

"Thanks," she whispered. And she blew a kiss toward the doll before running downstairs to join her friends.

MEET THE GIRLS FROM CABIN SIX IN

CAMP SUNNYSIDE FRIENDS SPECIAL:

CHRISTMAS REUNION	76270-6	($2.95 US/$3.50 Can)
(#9) THE NEW-AND-IMPROVED SARAH		
	76180-7	($2.95 US/$3.50 Can)
(#8) TOO MANY COUNSELORS	75913-6	($2.95 US/$3.50 Can)
(#7) A WITCH IN CABIN SIX	75912-8	($2.95 US/$3.50 Can)
(#6) KATIE STEALS THE SHOW	75910-1	($2.95 US/$3.50 Can)
(#5) LOOKING FOR TROUBLE	75909-8	($2.50 US/$2.95 Can)
(#4) NEW GIRL IN CABIN SIX	75703-6	($2.95 US/$3.50 Can)
(#3) COLOR WAR!	75702-8	($2.50 US/$2.95 Can)
(#2) CABIN SIX PLAYS CUPID	75701-X	($2.50 US/$2.95 Can)
(#1) NO BOYS ALLOWED!	75700-1	($2.50 US/$2.95 Can)
MY CAMP MEMORY BOOK	76081-9	($5.95 US/$7.95 Can)

EXTRA! EXTRA!
Read All About It in...

THE TREEHOUSE TIMES

(#8) THE GREAT RIP-OFF
75902-0 ($2.95 US/$3.50 Can)

(#7) RATS! 75901-2 ($2.95 US/$3.50 Can)

(#6) THE PRESS MESS
75900-4 ($2.95 US/$3.50 Can)

(#5) DAPHNE TAKES CHARGE
75899-7 ($2.95 US/$3.50 Can)

(#4) FIRST COURSE: TROUBLE
75783-4 ($2.50 US/$2.95 Can)

(#3) SPAGHETTI BREATH
75782-6 ($2.50 US/$2.95 Can)

(#2) THE KICKBALL CRISIS
75781-8 ($2.50 US/$2.95 Can)

(#1) UNDER 12 NOT ALLOWED
75780-X ($2.50 US/$2.95 Can)